HAUNTING
OF LaBelle

Back to Hell

J. THAYER MCKINNEY

"Haunting of LaBelle was a fast moving story that carried over from Grave Vengeance, Esther's Story. I really liked the way the books tied together. The author was very descriptive of the plantation and it didn't take much imagination to picture how beautiful it was. I couldn't lay it down, it was that interesting! I enjoyed the way the characters interacted with the spirits. I can assure it is a must read and will not disappoint you."

~ Carole

"J. Thayer McKinney has done a splendid job yet again with the Haunting of LaBelle. For anyone who enjoys reading about spirits and paranormal activity, won't want to miss this story – from bygone eras, southern plantations, to realizing your eyes aren't playing tricks will spellbind the reader to be compelled to finish this book."

~ M. M. Schmidt, author, When Angels Fly

"An intricate ghostly tale of past events whose effects ripple thru time."

~ Pamela S.

"Loved the book, if I hadn't read the first one [Grave Vengeance: Esther's Story] I would have been a little lost with the characters--I love to use my imagination and after reading both books, I can still imagine everything in them, kind of like listening to the radio when I was a little girl and using my imagination, thank you."

~ Linda Beaver Davis

Copyright © 2014 J. Thayer McKinney
All Rights Reserved
ISBN-13: 978-0692220115
ISBN-10: 0692220119

Cover Design and Interior Formatting by
Wicked Book Covers
www.wickedbookcovers.com

Second Edition 2014

Published and Printed in the United States of America by

Cedar Loft Productions
www.cedarloftproductions.com
J & P Enterprises, LLC

Prologue

August 1863

While Sam and Luke slowly dragged the three unconscious men to the back door, Belle made sure no one was out back at the cabins or outhouses. She didn't want anyone to see what was about to happen. She knew why Essie was going to do this but didn't agree this was the best way. She thought the sheriff should take care of outlaws.

Belle looked over at Sarah's cabin and saw that it was dark and Sarah wasn't sitting on her porch. Sam, Belle's bar keeper, was accustomed to dragging drunken customers out back to sober up and the other customers seldom paid any attention. Tonight was no exception. Everyone continued drinking and talking with the girls as if nothing was happening.

Sarah must have already gone to bed, Belle said to herself as she motioned for Sam and Luke to drag the men outside.

She didn't want Sarah to see what was going happening. Sarah was a religious woman and might not understand even though these same men murdered her husband, Jake, a few months before.

Jake was one of Belle's slaves and the three men decided to get rid of what they called a varmint. Before Belle or Sam could do anything, they grabbed Jake, took him out back and hanged him from a nearby tree. When Luke, another slave, saw what was happening, he quickly took the other slaves to hide in the barn.

Since her husband Jake had been murdered, Sarah didn't like staying up after the sun went down because that's when she missed him most. She and Jake used to sit on the porch from sunset until bedtime talking and listening to the night sounds. Now that he was gone, she just couldn't bear to sit on the porch in the evenings.

Before she had gotten to sleep, she heard a commotion over near Belle's Place. It sounded like Luke and Sam but she couldn't be sure so she got up and peeked out her window. She saw Luke and Sam dragging men out the back door of the saloon. There were three in all and they were laid side by side a ways from the building, near where Belle was standing. Soon Essie came out. *I wonder what's goin' on. Those men look dead but I cain't tell from here,* Sarah said to herself.

"Luke, you and Sam take the men out by the hog pen, take off all their clothes, and tie 'em up good," Essie instructed.

2

"I'll watch the saloon and make sure no one comes out back," Belle said. "Sarah seems to already be in bed so she won't see what's going on."

As they pulled the men one by one out to the hog pen Sarah moved to one of the back windows so she could see what they were doing. The moon was full making it almost as bright as day so she had no trouble seeing them but was sure they couldn't see her.

"Tie their hands an arms over their heads an tie their legs together," Essie told Luke and Sam. "I'm gonna get some planks to tie them to then I want ya to hoist 'em up on the feedin' platform and lean 'em agin the fence."

"Are ya sure bout this, Essie?" Luke asked.

"Yes, but if you don't wanna help, I understand."

"I'll help, jist wanna be sure ya know what ya be doin'."

"I know what I'm doin' and I mean to finish 'em off!"

"Us get 'em hoisted up, Sam, afore they come to," Luke said. "They's gonna be mean as snakes when they wake up."

Oh Lordy, what they got in mind? Lord have mercy, Sarah thought as she stood watching and wringing her hands.

Sarah watched as the men slowly came to. Essie was saying something to them but Sarah couldn't make out what she was saying. When she stopped talking, she whipped the men with a whip, then one by one tortured each of them. After she tortured each one and before

3

they died, she helped Sam and Luke push them into the pen for the hogs to eat alive.

Oh dear, I see dark evil surroundin' those men. They's gonna be big trouble, bad trouble.

Sarah waited until Essie, Luke and Sam went back to the saloon before leaving the window. She slowly walked to the fireplace and took down a small wooden box that was sitting on the mantle. She opened the box and took out several small beads, blessed them and put them in the pocket of her night dress. The beads were from her Creole grandmother and were quite powerful.

She put on her shoes and shawl and slowly walked out to the hog pen. When she got there, she could feel the evil. It seemed to surround her with its darkness. She carefully climbed up on the feeding platform and took the beads out of her pocket. The beads vibrated violently against her hand. She had to hold tight to them to keep them from falling to the ground.

Just then the earth where the men had died started shaking and a wide crevice opened. She heard the most evil laugher she had ever heard coming from underground. The ground was shaking so hard she had to hold onto the fence to keep from falling into the pen. With one hand, she slowly dropped the beads one by one into the crevice. The ground shook violently, the laugher turned to screams and the crevice suddenly closed.

She no longer felt the evil and was satisfied their spirits were sealed until someone opened the ground. She said a silent prayer as an additional precaution then climbed down from the feeding platform.

She started back to her cabin when she saw Jake's spirit. At first she was frightened but he put his arm around her and went back to the cabin with her.

"Jake, I'm so glad to see you. Please stay," she said after she calmed down.

"I cain't stay, Sarah but I kin rest in peace now that the men who killt me are dead and theys spirits be sealed," Jake's spirit told her.

"Oh, Jake, I be along with ya shortly," Sarah said through her tears. "As soon as my work here is done."

"Take you time, I be awaitin' fer ya," Jake said as he disappeared.

Sarah went into her cabin and slept the best she had since Jake died. She felt comfort in knowing Jake was all right and waiting for her. She just hoped it wouldn't be too long before she joined him.

The next day, she went about her chores with a smile on her face and she hummed a tune that Jake used to sing.

"I declare Miz Sarah, you be mighty happy today," Luke said as he fetched in fire wood for the kitchen stove.

"I be happy as can be, I seed Jake las night an he's awaitin' fer me in the hereafter."

Chapter 1

Debra Baxter was sitting at her desk at Baxter Properties. She had a concerned look on her face as she spoke with her client. Cory Jenkins was sitting in the chair across from her and was visibly upset. His property, LaBelle Mansion, had been listed with the real estate company for five years with no sale and essentially no interest in a sale. It was a prime piece of real estate but seemed to have no sales value. She had never had a listing that didn't at least attract a few potential buyers.

Debra had owned Baxter Properties for ten years and was accustomed to dealing with unhappy clients but Cory was a high priority and she worried about losing him as a client. A sale of this property would bring in quite a hefty commission for the company and the listing agent.

"Are you promoting my property or just sitting on it?" he demanded.

"We've been advertising it in the property books, online and in the newspapers from day one," Debra assured him. "There's an open house there this weekend and we've aggressively advertised that. It seems no one is interested and I'm not sure why. The price is certainly competitive if not low for the type of property."

"My wife is adamant about selling and the sooner the better. She wants shed of this property no matter what. It's been five years now and we need to either sell it or give it away!"

He remembered back to that day when he found his mother-in-law in the carriage house. Things hadn't been the same since and he was sure it was because of something that existed on the property.

Five years ago, his mother-in-law, JoAnne was a happy go-lucky artist who didn't act near her seventy years. JoAnne came to visit Cory and his wife, Jill, for a few weeks and decided to set up a small art studio in the carriage house while she was there. She spent hours painting getting ready for a show at the Castle Art Gallery in northern Virginia. The show was featuring her work all during October and she was excited because it meant she was finally being recognized as an artist.

One afternoon, Cory and Jill had business in town so JoAnne took the opportunity to paint without interruptions. She took a pitcher of iced tea and some cookies out to the carriage house, turned on her favorite music and proceeded to paint. Sometime in the late afternoon, she thought she heard muffled laughter so she went to the door thinking Jill and Cory had returned and were stopping by to check on her. When she looked out, she didn't see anything except what appeared to be shadows swirling around. *My goodness, my eyes are playing tricks on me, maybe I should stop for a while and have some tea,* she thought with a smile. She poured a glass of tea and settled into her chair to admire the work she had done so far.

As she sat sipping her tea, the laughter grew louder and she saw the shadows fly though the wall. They swirled around the room, slowly at first and then faster and faster as they turned darker and darker. The laughter was soon almost unbearably loud and JoAnne dropped her glass of tea and put her hands to her ears to try to stop the noise. To her surprise, she was unable to get up from the chair. Frantically she looked around the room but all she could see were the shadows swirling. Soon the shadows stopped swirling and seemed to be standing beside her canvas. She couldn't make out features, just dark images. She looked at her canvas and where her painting should have been were three grotesque faces that seemed to be in agony. One appeared to have no hair and the other two seemed to have long dark hair and beards. One of the faces with a beard had a triangle shaped scar on its cheek. Soon the look of agony on the faces was replaced by evil grins and the eyes seemed to penetrate into JoAnne's brain. She closed her eyes tightly to blot out the horrifying images.

Once again the shadows started swirling around the room and the laughter began again, getting louder and louder. JoAnne tried to scream but no sound would come from her throat. She just sat there with her hands over her ears and her eyes clamped tightly shut. She sat for what seemed like hours and finally she seemed to pass out.

When she came to, her hands were still over her ears but the shadows and the laughter were gone. She looked out the small window and saw that it was dark outside. The room was dark with only the light of the moon to illuminate it. She saw car lights coming up the drive but was unable to move. The car pulled up to the carriage house and she heard the doors close as both Cory and Jill got out. *Please come help me*, she whispered but the words wouldn't come out. She felt so helpless and was so frightened.

"I wonder what Mom has been up to while we've been gone," JoAnne heard her daughter say.

"I don't know but it's strange, there's no light in the house or the carriage house," Cory said with a concerned tone.

"MOM, MOM, are you alright," Jill screamed as she ran towards the house.

"She's not answering," she screamed to Cory. "Look in the carriage house while I look around the house."

Jill frantically ran from room to room calling for her mother.

10

Cory opened the door to the carriage house and went to the studio. When he walked in the door, he switched on the light and saw JoAnne sitting in the chair.

"JoAnne, are you okay?" he asked as he started to move closer to her.

When she didn't move or answer, he went to her and saw something was terribly wrong.

"JoAnne, what's wrong?" he shouted.

She just shook her head as tears ran down her cheeks. Her naturally auburn hair was completely white. "JoAnne, what happened here?" Cory pleaded but she just shook her head.

He helped her back to the house and into a chair. Jill saw her mother and almost fainted. She had never seen her mother look so horrible.

"Mom, what happened?" she screamed but JoAnne just shook her head.

"Get her some whiskey," Jill told Cory.

"Here JoAnne, drink this," he said as he handed her a small glass about a quarter full of whiskey. She drank it in one gulp and fell back in the chair and immediately went to sleep.

"Cory, look at her, how did her hair turn white?" Jill whispered to Cory.

"I don't know but something must have badly frightened her."

They sat with JoAnne all night until she awoke around five the next morning.

She still had a wild look in her eyes and wouldn't talk about what had happened.

"I want to leave this place now," she quietly insisted, "and I'm never coming back here."

"Mom what happened?" Jill pleaded.

"I don't want to ever talk about it. Just take me home."

"Okay, I'll get your paint and paintings while you and Jill pack your things," Cory told her.

"Leave the paintings, I don't want them or the paint. I'm never going to paint again and that's that."

"Mom, you can't mean that, what about the art show?"

"I'm not painting anymore and that's final."

"All right Mom, whatever you want. Let's gather your things together," Jill said sadly.

"Cory, if Mom doesn't want to be here then neither do I. Something terrible happened and I don't want to live here anymore," Jill told him. "I'll pack some of my things and stay with Mom while you put this place on the market and sell or give away the furnishing. I don't want those either, they'll never fit in another house and besides they will just remind me of tonight.

Cory knew better than to try to change her mind because once Jill made a decision, she didn't go back.

They went upstairs while JoAnne packed her belongings. Jill packed a few of things she would need until they could make a permanent move. Once both had finished packing, they slowly came back downstairs to the living room.

"Cory, we're all packed. I'll help you bring the suitcases down and then I'll sit with Mom while you pack the car."

He loaded the back of the SUV with both women's belongings, locked the house and headed to JoAnne's house. Even though he was leery of being here alone, Cory decided come back the next day and start clearing the place and get it ready to sell.

A few days later, he stopped by Baxter Properties to list the property for sale. Debra looked at the property and listed it herself since Cory insisted on doing business with her. Eventually she talked him into letting her pass the listing to one of the salespeople since she didn't actively sell, she just managed the office.

Even though she wasn't actively involved, she promised to oversee the listing to be sure it got adequate exposure. She gave Cory the name and phone number of an auctioneer so he could set up a sale of the household furniture and goods. She was sure their furnishings would sell quickly.

A sale was scheduled for two weeks from Saturday so Cory decided to stay at the house until afterwards. He was uncomfortable staying there but found nothing unusual even in the nighttime hours. *I wonder what could have spooked JoAnne,* he thought to himself. He had heard the rumors about the place being haunted but that was hogwash as far as he was concerned.

13

"Cory, are you alright?" Debra questioned when Cory seemed to be off in another world. It worried Debra but she didn't let on to Cory.

"Yes, I'm sorry, just thinking about the night JoAnne went crazy out at that place. You know she went completely over the edge a few days after she left, don't you?"

"No, I'm so sorry. This must have been difficult for you and Jill."

"I think it might have been easier if I knew what happened that night but I guess I'll never know. Jill's mother died just a couple of weeks after leaving that place. Overnight, she turned from a vibrant, healthy woman to a frail, sickly old lady. There's something awful on that place and we can't live there any longer."

"So what do you propose we do to sell?" Debra asked. "I've done everything I can think of and to be honest, your place should have sold within a few weeks."

"I'm going to lower the price. I know that's cutting into your commission but I have to get shed of this albatross. Jill is adamant about not keeping it any longer even if we have to give it away."

"Let's see how the open house goes this weekend and take it from there," Debra suggested. "I'll talk to Jett tomorrow afternoon to see if she had any prospects."

"Thanks, Debra, I'll wait to hear from you but I want this sold or given away by the end of the month. You know we don't need the money but we do need the peace of mind. Even if you give it away, I'll see that you get the commission on the original asking price."

Cory got up, shook hands with Debra and left the office.

Debra pushed the speed dial button for Jett's cell phone but it went to voice mail. She knew Jett wouldn't answer her phone if she was with a client so this was a good sign. She left a message to call as soon as she got the message no matter what time it was.

Chapter 2

Jett Anthony reluctantly agreed to hold an open house at LaBelle Mansion for the coming weekend. The property had been listed with Baxter Properties for almost five years with little or no interest from buyers. The seller had reduced his price several times trying to entice a sale but with no luck. The gossip around town was that the property was haunted but Jett doesn't believe in ghosts. All the same, she had a bad feeling about being out there all alone.

Jett was given the listing just after she signed on as an agent a year ago. The previous listing agent disappeared after showing the property last August. No one thought foul play since he wasn't the most reliable person at the agency and he hadn't listed any immediate family in his personnel file. Most thought he just moved on to something better and didn't think much about his disappearance. Debra, the owner of Baxter Properties thought about notifying the sheriff but had nothing to tell him. She could have filed a missing person's report but no one actually missed him and that would cause a lot of unnecessary work and expense for the sheriff.

Jett arrived at the property a little after ten on Saturday morning. She wandered around the house to make sure everything was in place and as a precaution, she made sure all the doors and windows were locked.

She brought a book with her so she sat on the front porch reading and hoping someone would stop by. It was now getting close to two in the afternoon and still no visitors. She felt uneasy all day and at times thought she saw shadows milling around.

"Get hold of yourself," she said under her breath. "There's no such thing as ghosts. Your imagination is getting the best of you and your eyes are playing tricks."

Still, she wished someone would show up or she could just pack up and leave but according to the contract, she had to stay until 4:00. Her boss wouldn't want someone showing up to see the property only to find no one there to show it. She turned her radio up a little louder as she sat in the swing reading.

She wished she had a beer or a bottle of wine but that would have to wait until she got back to her apartment. She had been at the house other times with no ill effects but today, she somehow felt uneasy being here. Almost like there was a dark cloud of doom and gloom that she couldn't explain. She couldn't figure out why she felt so strange. This feeling was all new to her.

She wished her eyes would quit playing tricks on her. It seemed no matter where she looked, three shadows darted just out of her sight. She squeezed her eyes shut and when she opened them, the shadows were still there but just for an instant.

This is crazy, there's no such thing a ghosts! This place is driving me crazy!

She had just settled back to read when her phone rang. She answered but all she heard was static. She started to make a call to Debra but her phone showed no service.

What's going on, I had full service a few minutes ago. I hope the cell site didn't go down. I sure hate to be way out here all day with no phone, she thought to herself. She kept checking her phone but it still had no service.

She got up and paced back and forth on the porch wanting to just pack up and leave but knew she might lose her job if she did. She was starting to feel frightened and wasn't sure how much more she could stand.

* * *

Elana Palmer was sitting in the living room of the apartment she shared with her husband Scott. The apartment was small, just three rooms and a bath. This might have been plenty big enough if they didn't have so much stuff. Elana couldn't stand clutter but it was impossible to find a place for all their belongings. As soon as she reached her 30th birthday, her trust fund would be available and she was determined to buy a house, a huge house.

Elana was a petite woman with her blond hair cut in a pixie style that made her look even smaller and definitely younger than her 29 years. She mostly dressed in blue jeans, white tees and flip-flops unless Scott decided to take her to one of his corporate functions. Then she dressed as the trophy wife. Scott liked to put on airs for his colleagues and she was willing to go along just for the fun of it even though she disliked dressing up.

Elana was finishing studies for her Master's in psychology and wanted to open a couple's retreat. She had big plans of becoming an authority in sexuality and how to help couples get in touch with their inner feelings toward each other. She planned to start her PhD dissertation next.

She wandered around the tiny apartment wondering what to do since she didn't know when Scott might return. Sometimes when he was in one of his moods, he was gone for hours.

"Fuck it," Elana said to no one in particular. "I'm getting out of here."

Scott had stormed out an hour or so ago so she decided she would do the same. Normally they got along just fine but the past couple of weeks had been particularly difficult for them both. Scott was in line for a promotion at work and Elana was trying to finish her classes for her degree even though she wouldn't graduate until next May. Both were on edge and at each other's throats for no reason.

She went out, put the top down on her old convertible and backed out of her parking spot. It was past lunch time so she stopped at the corner convenient store for a chili dog, chips and a drink. She would love to have a six pack of beer but didn't need a DUI right now. *Maybe I'll stop on my way home and pick up some beer for this evening.*

After eating her lunch, Elana opened a soda and backed out of the parking lot and turned right towards the valley. The road was narrow and winding but so peaceful and not much traffic at all. She loved the valley with the mountains on each side and the lazy river meandering through the fields. There were stately old mansions and plantations dotting the landscape and several remained much the same as they had been years ago.

She dreamed of owning a large old mansion or plantation but never in her wildest dreams did she think it would ever happen. Maybe she would pass an open house and do some daydreaming. Just then she spotted a real estate sign that said ***Beautiful LaBelle Mansion OPEN HOUSE SATURDAY AND SUNDAY!*** How lucky could she get?

She turned into the drive and drove through a canopy of trees lining both sides. At the end of the drive was a beautiful old mansion. A walkway led to the steps that went up to the huge porch that extended across the front of the house. The front of the house looked so welcoming, especially the large front door.

"Oh my god," Elana said out loud, "my dream house!"

She pulled into a space beside an SUV that obviously belonged to the real estate agent. She slowly got out and took in the splendor of the house and the surroundings. It looked so elegant that Elana couldn't believe it was on the market. *I'd never sell this place if I owned it.*

"Put your eyes back in your head and come on up," a friendly voice beckoned.

"This is just too beautiful!" Elana gushed as she climbed the steps to the porch.

"Needs a bit of work but it is beautiful. I'm Jett Anthony," the real estate agent said as she offered her hand to Elana.

Jett was a tall, heavy set woman with bright red hair pulled back into a pony tail. She wore a pink polyester pants suit that clashed terribly with her red hair. Her nails were painted bright red as were her full lips. To say Jett was crude was an understatement but she was very personable and Elana immediately decided she liked her.

"Hi, I'm Elana Palmer. I hope you don't mind but I'm just looking. No way on earth I could afford something this elegant."

"You might be surprised. The owner wants to sell. The starting price is under $450,000 and he hasn't had any interest shown yet."

"You're kidding."

"No. I'm certainly not. Normally I wouldn't give that much information but I need another sale before the end of the month to make my quota so I'm all mouth."

"How much land is with it?" Elana inquired.

"A hundred or so acres, all fenced and mostly level," Jett answered after looking at her listing papers. "It has the mansion, a smaller house, the large building that was used as a school for women and several outbuildings. Oh and the school was used as a whore house during the Civil War. Some history, huh?"

"Interesting. So how old is the house?"

"The mansion and small house were built just after the Civil War but the school was built in the late 1700s or early 1800s. I'm not sure about the outbuildings.

"According to the history I have, the Madam that owned the brothel fell in love with a Confederate officer and after the war they got married.

He didn't want to operate a brothel so they turned it into a school for young women where the girls who worked for Belle could receive an education. He built the mansion for his bride and the smaller house for the caretakers of the school. At one time there were a few log cabins where slaves had lived but those have long since been destroyed."

"What a lovely story. I've dreamed of opening a couples retreat and the history of this place is perfect," Elana mused.

My trust fund will be available soon, Elana thought to herself. *I hope it's enough to put a down payment on this*. Her mind was buzzing with the possibilities.

Jett smiled as she started to see that Elana was most definitely interested. She just hoped nothing would happen to spoil a sale if she truly was thinking about buying.

"What all do you want to see?" Jett asked. "I'm not sure that we'll get to everything this afternoon but we can sure try."

"Let's look at everything," Elana said excitedly.

"We'll start with the mansion since we're already here and then if there's time, we'll look at the rest of the buildings," Jett said. She was relieved she had finally stopped seeing the shadows. "I'll be back here tomorrow if we don't get to all of them today."

"That's wonderful, my husband might be able to come back with me tomorrow!"

"How about a couple of cookies and some soda before we get started? I brought enough for a small army and it doesn't look like anyone else is going to show up."

"Sounds good, the cookies look delicious and I'm kind of thirsty. Okay if I take them with me while we look?"

"Sure."

"The room we are in now is the main foyer. As you can see, there are doors leading to the other rooms on the main floor and a grand stairway leading to the second floor. We'll tour the main floor first," Jett said in her professional voice.

"I love that stairway, it's so elegant!" Elana exclaimed. "It reminds me of the stairways in movies about the south."

"Yes, it is a beauty. The entire mansion has been remodeled several times and all of the owners kept the stairway as original as possible. The current owner did the most work. It's a shame he put all that time and money into it and now wants to sell."

"You'll notice that all the rooms have doors leading to the next room along with a door into the foyer. There are twelve rooms, the foyer and six baths."

They went through the doorway at the bottom of the stairs, just beyond the main door. The doorway was two double doors with windows.

"This room is the ballroom and the largest room in the house. It's said that many gala events were hosted in this room."

The room had two beautiful crystal chandeliers, a fireplace, and an ornate ceiling. It had been modernized with electrical outlets and the chandeliers were now electric.

"This would make a super gathering room for entertaining," Elana said as she took in the beauty of the room.

"There's a smaller room off this room that could be used as a sitting room. I believe when the house was built, it was a side entrance into the ballroom. There's another room just like this one on the parlor side," Jett offered as they went through double glass doors to a smaller room."

"These would make lovely sitting rooms to just enjoy relaxing and reading."

"The next room is the dining room," Jett said as they walked through the door at the rear of the ballroom. "There's no furniture in any of the rooms but I think you can get a feel of how each room might look with your own personal touches."

The dining room was no disappointment. It had a large fireplace at on end, wainscoting around the walls, an ornate ceiling and a crystal chandelier. The floor was hardwood the same as the ballroom. It was large enough for the dinner parties Elana wanted to host with room to spare.

"This door leads to a small hallway with a powder room and access to the kitchen. The kitchen is in an extension of the house so the cooking wouldn't cause too much heat during the summer months.

There are two rooms and a bath for each over the kitchen. Probably the cook and butler lived in those rooms," Jett told her as they walked into the hallway.

The powder room was small and functional but unimpressive. The kitchen, however, was a cook's dream. A huge fireplace was at one end and it had been remodeled into a marvelous array of cupboards, cabinets, counter tops, sinks, storage and so much more. On one side of the room was a door to the stairs going up to the second floor. Near the fireplace was a laundry room with a door that led outside.

Upstairs were two large rooms, each with a full bath. The rooms would serve nicely as an apartment for a live in housekeeper if Elana decided to buy the property. She was already planning ahead with the possibilities.

Elana hated to leave the kitchen but knew they had to move along with the tour since it was getting late.

They went back into the small hallway and through a door into the parlor. It too had a fireplace, ornate ceiling and hardwood floors. This room had no ceiling light but there were plenty of electrical outlets for lamps. Next to the parlor was a sitting room that looked similar to the parlor. The sitting room had a smaller room off to the side that led to the outside, the same as the one off the ballroom.

After touring the first floor, they returned to the foyer. Brett glanced around and was relieved when she didn't see any shadows lurking in the corners. *I wonder if there are ghosts or if I'm really going crazy.*

So, what do you think so far?" Jett asked.

"It's fabulous!" Elana exclaimed.

"Let's go upstairs and then take a look outside and at the other house. I think you'll fall in love with the master bedroom."

At the top of the stairs, Jett opened the door to a room directly above the ballroom. There was a fireplace in this room, the same ornate ceiling as in the rest of the house, hardwood floors, and a crystal chandelier.

At the back end of the room was an archway with a garden tub on one side and a double shower on the other. A double sink was beyond the tub and a small room with the toilet and a bidet was beyond the shower.

"Unbelievable!" Elana exclaimed as she checked out the bidet. "I can't believe this place wasn't sold a long time ago."

They left the master bedroom and looked at the four other bed rooms and baths. These rooms were typical of an older home but were much larger than Elana expected and each had a fireplace.

After they had walked through the entire house, Jett and Elana went out onto the front porch.

"I just can't believe no one has bought this place. It's beautiful and has so many possibilities."

"Oh, it's been sold several times but for one reason or another it goes back on the market. Could be the upkeep is too much or maybe it's because it's so far away from other neighbors. Or, there are rumors that it's haunted," Jett said with a grin.

"Oh my goodness, I don't believe in ghosts. That's just plain silly. I haven't seen any ghosties today, have you?"

"Not that I know of," Jett replied as she crossed her fingers remembering the strange shadows she had seen earlier. She looked around almost expecting to see the shadows once again and was relieved when it appeared they were gone.

"Do you want some more cookies and soda before we look at the rest of the property?" Jett asked.

"Yeah, I'll grab a couple of cookies and a soda to carry with me. We need to move right along. It's getting late."

"We'll only peek in the old school building because it's in need of repairs and I don't want any accidents. You can get a feel for it and if you're interested, we can do a thorough tour tomorrow or at a later time."

"That's fine, we really don't have to go through the other house either. I would like to take a quick peek into the school though. Most of my interest is in the large house and the school building. Those are where I would be spending most of my time if we bought the place."

They walked down the steps from the front porch toward the school. At the bottom of the steps Elana saw a small metal object sticking out of the ground. It looked like a scraper with a ball on each side of the scraper part.

"What's this?" she asked Jett. "It looks really old."

"That's a boot scraper to scrape the mud off boots before going into the house. There's a couple over at the old school too."

"Well that's clever."

"Yes and dangerous. Can you imagine falling on that thing? I'm sure it would leave a nasty cut and a terrible scar."

"Wonder how many have battle scars from it?" Elana laughed.

They walked across the driveway and yard to the rear entrance of the school building. Jett unlocked the door and pushed it open. They peered down a short hallway with several open doors. Just opposite of the outside door was a large room with what looked like a bar or countertop just barely in sight.

"Let's walk around to the front door and peek in that one too." Jett said.

The building was huge, much larger than Elana had first thought.

Before I even think about making an offer, I'll want to get an estimate on remodeling this bad boy, she thought to herself.

At the front of the building was a long porch with steps leading up to the front door. Elana noticed these steps had a boot scraper on each side of the bottom step.

"Be careful, the steps and porch are rickety," Jett cautioned as her phone rang.

"Aren't you going to answer that?" Elana asked.

"No, I don't take calls when I'm with a client," Jett said wondering how she suddenly had service.

"I'm not a client yet," Elana laughed.

"Not yet but maybe soon," Jett smiled as she unlocked and opened the door into a large room with a magnificent circular stairway leading to the second floor. Elana thought it was a shame to let such a beautiful building fall to decay. They walked towards the rear of the house and Elana saw the beautiful old bar. It was in need of some refurbishing but it was still beautiful.

"We can peek at the rooms downstairs and then upstairs if you'd like," Jett said.

"Let's just take a look downstairs today and then do a thorough tour when there's more time. Can we walk around the other side of the building on the way back to the house?" Elana asked.

"Sure, you'll be able to see the carriage house from there. We can go out the kitchen door."

As they stepped onto the side porch, Jett thought she saw shadows down at the carriage house but didn't say a word to Elana. *If she doesn't see them, I'm not going to call attention.*

"That's the carriage house at the end of the driveway. It was added a long time after the original owners were gone. I think there used to be a hog pen there. It's said the woman who owned the brothel raised hogs to sell to the Union and Confederate troops during the war," Jett told Elana.

Jett looked at her watch and said, "We better wrap this up, it's almost time for me to get back to the office."

When they got back to the house Jett gave Elana her card and told her to call if she wanted to see the place again and definitely to call if she wanted to make an offer.

Elana offered to help Jett pack her things but she reluctantly declined. She really didn't want to stay there alone but she didn't feel it was professional to allow a client to help load the car.

"I'm only going to pack a few things since I'm going to be here again tomorrow bright and early. No need to do extra work. I don't think there are mice or anything that might bother my things."

"It was so nice meeting you Jett and I hope I can get Scott to come back out tomorrow for another look around."

Elana climbed into her car, backed out of the parking space and waved as she drove down the drive to the main road.

Jett watched her until she was out of sight and then slowly walked up the steps to the house to start gathering up her supplies. She now wished she would have taken Elana up on her offer to help.

I sure wish I was far, far away from here, she thought as she was packing a few things to carry to her car.

She only had two trips to make to her car before she had everything that she planned to take loaded. On her second trip into the house she thought she heard muffled laughter.

"Is anyone there?" she inquired. "Come on, if someone is in here, come out or I'm calling the sheriff."

Then she saw three dark shadows hovering in the foyer. She could barely make out the features but as she looked at them they materialized more. One had no hair and the other two had long hair and beards. The largest of the three had what looked like a triangular scar on one cheek. All three were laughing an evil laugh that penetrated into Jett's brain like a knife cutting into crisp bread.

When she finally realized what she was seeing, she screamed and ran out of the house and down the steps. When she got almost to the bottom step she lost her balance and fell face first into the grass beside the steps. Her neck hit the scraper part of the boot scraper severing her carotid artery. She tried to get up but was only able to turn a bit but enough that she could see the three ghosts. As she lay there with blood gushing from her wound and her life slipping away she heard them roaring with laughter as they swirled around her. As she drew her last breath, the three ghosts swirled around her once more then flew to a spot behind the carriage house and were gone.

Late that evening when Debra hadn't yet heard from Jett, she tried her cell phone again. It went to voice mail once again. *That's strange*, Debra thought, *Jett should be answering or should have returned my call by now.* This was unlike Jett and was starting to worry Debra.

Chapter 3

Elana's mind was racing as she left the property and headed back home. She couldn't wait to tell Scott about her find and hoped he was home and in a better mood. He had been a bit testy since he found out he was up for the promotion. She understood he was under a lot of pressure with his job but she was under pressure too.

She was just a couple of weeks away from finishing studies for her Master's degree and finals were next week. Once she finished her studies, she would be eligible for an internship and would begin her PhD dissertation. She was concerned about whether or not she had made the right decision in her career choice but it was too late to change her mind now.

She wanted to be a marriage and sex counselor and open a couple's retreat using the latest new age technology and treatments. Her main concern was if this type of practice would be accepted. As far as she knew, there were only a few counselors offering the services she wanted to offer and they were in the large cities. It would take a lot of work and preparation but she was sure she could do it.

Scott was a senior software developer with Askee and Markus Software Alliance and was in line for a promotion to executive vice president of development and the competition was fierce. Two others were also being considered for the promotion. Scott should have been a shoo-in but a few weeks ago he broke his arm playing racket ball and missed a few days of work.

The time off put him out of the loop so the others had an advantage. Now, he spent every minute he could at the office even though it meant staying in the city some nights. He was always home on weekends since company policy didn't permit working weekends, at least for now.

If he got the promotion, he would work whenever necessary and that included nights and weekends. Elana wasn't sure she wanted him to get the promotion but he wanted it just to prove to his father he was a success. His father thought anyone not in an executive position was an utter failure, especially a man.

I wonder if Scott would like Chinese for dinner, she thought to herself.

She was a mile or so from the Chinese carry-out and decided to pick up some orange chicken, General Tso's chicken, fried rice and Lo Mein noodles. If Scott wasn't hungry or not home, she could save the leftovers. She also decided to pick up a bottle of wine and a strawberry cheesecake for desert.

When Elana pulled into the parking lot for their apartment, she was relieved to see Scott's car in its parking space.

Oh, good, Scott's home. I hope he's in a good mood, she thought to herself.

She pulled into her parking space beside Scott's car, got her purse and the bags of food and walked up the steps to their apartment. She rang the bell since she couldn't get her keys without putting down her bags. Scott opened the door and gave her a big grin.

"Hey gorgeous, where've you been?" he asked still grinning.

His grin was what Elana had first noticed when she met Scott four years ago, that and his black hair and blue eyes. She had never seen such a handsome man and was surprised when he walked right up to her and started talking. It was love at first sight for both of them. They were married three months later.

"Well, you're in a better mood."

"Yep, and we're going to celebrate!"

"What are we celebrating?"

"I got a call from Jeff to meet him and Mr. Reynolds first thing Monday morning to sign the papers for the executive vice-president of development position. The board had an emergency meeting this morning and voted me in. This means we can start looking for a house and get out of this apartment."

"Fantastic, I brought Chinese, wine and a strawberry cheesecake so let's celebrate right here."

"And afterward, we can really celebrate if you know what I mean," he said as he winked and patted her on the behind.

"Tease," she whispered as she handed him the bags.

"Oh, I bought pizza on the way home so which do you want tonight? We can save the other for tomorrow night," Scott said as he walked into the tiny kitchen.

"Let's do pizza tonight, the Chinese will heat up better. And I have some stuff to tell you about my day too."

Scott got plates for the pizza and glasses for the wine as Elana opened the box and picked up some forks. She placed a couple of slices on each plate and poured the wine. They carried their food and drink to the couch and settled in to have supper and talk.

"Tell me about your day first," Scott said.

"I found the most spectacular house today. Well, it's actually a mansion on an old plantation. It's for sale and with my trust fund and your new job, we can certainly afford it!" As they ate, Elana filled him in on what she had seen and how beautiful it all was.

"Sounds fantastic!"

"It will still be open for show again tomorrow, can we go look at it together?"

"Sure, I don't have anything planned and it might be fun and if it's as good as you say, we might just make an offer. I want out of this dump now that I'm an execu-

38

tive," he said with a wink and a grin. "We can't entertain properly in a small apartment."

"This house has a beautiful dining room where we can host lavish dinner parties. Oh and did I tell you it's haunted?" Elana said with a chuckle.

"Awesome and our own resident ghost but you know I don't believe in ghosts."

"Me neither and I didn't see anything while I was there. I think it's just a reputation all old houses get. And, get this, the old building on the property was a whore house during the Civil War."

"This place just gets better and better. We have to go look at it. We'll grab some lunch at one of the fast food places and then drive over and spend all afternoon looking it over," Scott told her. "Now finish your pizza and wine and let's get to bed. I'll tell you all about my new job tomorrow."

Elana was so excited and she loved Scott so much right then. This property was what she had always dreamed of owning. As soon as they finished eating, she took their dishes to the kitchen and put them in the sink.

"Do you want some dessert before we turn in?"

"I had dessert in mind after we turn in," Scott grinned.

He grabbed her around the waist and half carried her to the little bedroom where he fell on the bed with her. They laughed and wrestled and then got serious. An hour or so later, they lay wrapped in each other's arms sound asleep. They awoke the next morning snuggled together. Even though they fought sometimes, they loved each other and always made up before going to sleep. Scott said they fought so much because the make-up sex was so good.

Scott nudged Elana, "hey sleepy head, time to get up."

"What time is it?" she asked as she stretched and yawned.

"A little after eight and we have a full day planned and we don't want to waste a minute of it."

After showers and breakfast, Elana was ready and eager to go back to the mansion.

"We'll get something for lunch on the way so we can take our time looking at the place," Scott said as he sipped his coffee. "Did you say there was a convenience store nearby?"

"There is and there's a quaint little seafood restaurant called Chips and Chowder on the way."

"Oh, that sounds good. A good bowl of clam chowder and chips would make a great lunch."

About 10:00, they were finally ready to leave. The property was only about an hour away so they should have plenty of time for a leisurely lunch.

"Let's take your car," Elana said as they were walking down the steps to the parking lot.

"Okay, I just got it filled up so we won't have to worry about getting gas. Where's this place from here?"

"It's on Highway 2 south near Cantor," Elana told him. "The restaurant is about five miles before we get to the property."

"We can fix up the old school building with a spa, indoor pool, meeting rooms, and meditation rooms downstairs and sleeping rooms for couples upstairs. There's a small house near the building that can serve as offices for both of us and maybe rooms for help to stay. I think the two rooms above the kitchen in the mansion would be a perfect apartment for a live-in housekeeper," Elana chattered excitedly.

"Whoa, slow down, we have to buy this place first," Scott laughed.

"Oh, I know you're going to love it as much as I do and we can certainly afford it now. Did I tell you the owner is asking a ridiculously low price and I might be able talk him down even more since it's been on the market for almost five years?"

"Okay, we'll look it over real good and if all looks all right, make an offer."

"Up ahead, the sign for Cantor," Elana said as she pointed to the large green highway sign.

"How in the world did you find this place?"

"Don't know, just was driving around and there it was. Fate maybe."

"Could be, we'll see."

Scott exited the Interstate and turned left onto Highway 2 towards Cantor. Elana was quiet, going over her plans in her mind and occasionally smiling to herself as she thought of all the possibilities. She hadn't been this happy in a long time. It seemed everything was finally coming together for her and Scott and she loved it.

"Looks like Chips and Chowder up ahead on the right," Scott said with a grin.

"Good, I'm getting hungry."

He pulled into the small gravel parking lot and parked near the door to the restaurant. The large front window had a huge, laughing clam painted on it. There was mooring across the front of the restaurant to simulate a boat dock with concrete pelicans and shells between the mooring and the building. Scott held the door for Elana and she squealed with delight as she walked into the restaurant. The tables were small and covered with blue checked oil cloth covers. Each had an oil lamp burning and fake gold coins sprinkled around the lamps. There was a long mahogany bar with a replica pirate ship behind. The waitresses were dressed in pirate suits as was the bartender.

"Oh, my gosh, this place is incredible!" Elana cried.

"It is quite impressive," Scott agreed.

They each ordered a bowl of clam chowder with chips, the house salad, lemonade and pie for desert. There was an old juke box in one corner so Elana decided to check it out.

"Does the juke box work?" she asked the waitress.

"Sure does and only takes a quarter for each song or five for a dollar but they are old songs."

"Give me a dollar," she told Scott.

She picked five songs that she had loved when she was much younger and sang along with a couple of them while waiting for their food. Scott just sat and grinned at her, half embarrassed and half proud. He did love to see her having fun.

Soon the waitress brought their food and they were amazed at the size of the bowl of chowder.

"I think we could have shared a bowl," Elana told Scott. "I'm not sure I can eat this much but I'm sure going to try."

"This is delicious, why haven't we found this place before now?" Scott asked.

"I don't know but we'll be back, that's for sure."

When they finished their meal and dessert, Scott left a $10.00 tip for the waitress and went to the register to pay the bill. Elana wandered around the restaurant looking at the pictures and other decorations making a mental note of those she really liked. She might want to use this décor in the couples retreat. She also noticed a picture of what looked like the old school building.

"How was everything?" the cashier inquired.

"Excellent," Scott told her. "We'll sure be back for more and will tell all our friends about this place."

"Glad you liked it and look forward to seeing you again soon," the cashier said with a smile as she handed him his change.

They got back in the car and Elana laid her head back in the seat. "I think its nappy time."

Scott laughed and said, "Oh yeah, a nap would be great about now. I'm stuffed,"

He backed out of the parking space, pulled onto the highway and headed for the mansion.

Chapter 4

When Debra didn't hear back from Jett by 10:00 that evening, she decided to call the sheriff and ask him to check her apartment to see if she was all right. Jett lived alone and didn't have any family near and was so busy with her real estate job, she didn't have any close friends.

"Joe, this is Deb, I'm kind of worried about Jett and wonder if you could drive by her apartment and see if everything's okay?"

"Sure, I'm about five minutes away and will let you know," he said. Joe was sort of sweet on Jett and had tried to get her to go out with him several times but Jett wasn't interested. Joe was persistent and hoped it was just a matter of time before she finally said yes.

A few minutes later he called Debra back and told her the apartment was dark and Jett's car wasn't in the parking lot.

"That's strange," Debra said trying to not sound too worried. "She had an open house at the LaBelle Mansion today and I haven't heard from her all day. I wonder if you would drive out by the mansion to see if she's still there. Maybe she has car trouble."

"Sure thing," Joe replied. "I should be there in about 20 minutes or so."

Joe drove up Highway 2 and saw the open house sign at the driveway into the mansion. He turned in and drove back to the parking area in front of the mansion and behind the old school building. When he got within sight of the house, he saw a car and was sure it was Jett's but took some precaution just in case it wasn't. He eased up to the lot and pulled in beside the car and sure enough it was Jett's SUV but he didn't see Jett anywhere.

Now where has that woman gotten off to, he wondered to himself. He waited in the car for a few minutes and looked things over as much as he could in the dark. There was a full moon but the trees blocked much of the light. His car lights shined onto the porch and he could see the front door was wide open but there didn't seem to be anyone around.

Joe got out of his vehicle, hand on his side arm, ready just in case he was surprised by someone, and walked over to Jett's car. There was no one in the driver's seat but Jett's purse was in the passenger's seat and the door was wide open. *Now that's strange,* he thought to himself as he walked to the front of the vehicle. That's when he saw her.

"Oh sweet Jesus," he screamed. "Jett, Jett, what happened?" But he got no response.

He went up the walk to where Jett laid and saw she was most certainly dead. She was lying with her head in the grass at the bottom of the steps and the rest of her body was on the steps. She was turned as if she had tried to get up. There was a pool of blood around her head and it looked as though her face had been eaten off by an animal. He wanted to turn and leave but knew he had to stay. *Oh, Jett, what happened to you? I wish I couldn't have been here to help you.*

He got on his radio, "Bobby, Dave, get your butts out to the LaBelle Mansion and bring the coroner."

"10-4, Joe, on our way," Bobby replied.

"I'm callin' the coroner now," Dave announced. "Sounds bad, what's wrong?"

"Can't tell you over the radio but you'll see when you get here. Now high tail it out here you two."

He looked around but saw no signs of struggle so he was certain Jett had taken a tumble and struck her head. He got his flashlight and walked up to the front door of the house and peered in. There were boxes and papers for the open house on the small table but nothing looked out of place.

Joe immediately called Deb. She was expecting his call and answered on the first ring. "Deb, I found Jett," he told her.

"Oh thank God," she said. "Is she alright? Where is she?"

"Oh Deb, it's awful, Jett's dead. Looks like she fell out here at the mansion and struck her head."

"Oh no, I'm coming out!"

"I don't think you should, it's not a pretty sight."

"I'm coming out. I'll be there as fast as I can. I just have to slip on my shoes and jacket."

Joe heard the sirens coming up the highway and in a few minutes saw the flashing lights as they turned in the driveway. There were two police cars and an ambulance.

"Bobby, you and Dave take a look around the place and see if you find anything unusual," the sheriff told the deputies. They each took a flashlight and left to walk around the grounds.

The coroner brought his bag and started examining the body. He looked at the face and said, "Oh dear, it looks like the animals have started on her."

He turned her over and saw the boot scraper and the wound on her neck. "It looks like she fell on the sharp edge of this boot scraper and cut her carotid artery and bled to death. I'd say she died around 5 or 5:30 this afternoon but will know for sure on all this when I get her back to the morgue."

Joe took a camera from his car and took several shots of the body and the surrounding area just in case there were problems later. He tried to always take pictures when he was called to an accident or crime scene.

"Sonny, bring the gurney over and let's get her out of here," the coroner called to the EMT that was with him.

Bobby and Dave returned and told the sheriff everything looked all right as far as they could tell.

48

"Joe, this looks like an accident so I don't see a reason for an autopsy, do you?" the coroner asked the sheriff.

"No, Bill, don't see any evidence of foul play here, just an unfortunate accident," Joe said shaking his head.

As the ambulance was pulling onto the highway, Debra was getting ready to turn in. She drove back to the house and parked beside the sheriff's car.

"What happened?" she called to the sheriff.

"It looks as though she tripped and fell on this boot scraper and cut her throat," he said obviously shaken.

"Oh shit, pull that damned thing out of there," Debra ordered. "I don't want any more accidents to happen here."

"What do you mean by any more accidents?" the sheriff asked as he took an evidence kit from his trunk. He took several pictures of the boot scraper and then put on a pair of gloves, pulled it from the ground, deposited it into an evidence bag, and sealed it.

"I don't really know of any accidents in the past but last year Mike Ranson had an open house here and we haven't heard from him since."

"Why didn't you report it? I could have done a thorough investigation."

"Well, Mike was always taking off so we didn't think much of it. He would be missing for a few days or even a few weeks and then all at once show up. He was a good salesman but unreliable. As I said we didn't think much about it and I eventually forgot until now."

"I really wish you would have reported it to me. Did he have any family or did any one report him missing?" the sheriff inquired.

"No and no. He didn't even have a girlfriend that I knew of."

"Well, he's probably relaxing on a beach somewhere so we'll not worry about it," the sheriff mused.

"Look at this mess," Deb said as she looked at all the blood. "Not too good for having an open house tomorrow."

"The boys and me will clean it up for you tonight before we leave," Joe said.

"Oh, thanks so much Joe, I'll stick around and help."

"Let's get this mess cleaned up. Did either of you see a hose when you walked around the house?"

"Yes, there's one at the back of the house. Let's look and see if there's a faucet here in front. I doubt it's long enough to reach."

"Here's one," Dave called from beside the porch. "Bobby, bring the hose around and we'll get what we can."

"Deb, you need to go on home. While the boys are cleaning up, I'm going to look around a bit more before we leave. I'm going to call the tow truck to pick up Jett's car so I'll want to be here when it arrives too."

"I'll stay with you," Debra said as she started up the steps to the house. "As bad as I hate to, I'm going to come back in the morning for the Sunday open house so I want to be sure everything looks all right."

"Are you sure you want to do that? Can't one of the other agents do that?" Joe asked as he called the towing service.

"No, under the circumstances, I need to be here. The seller is getting pretty testy about it not selling and this thing with Jett will be the icing on the cake. I'm going to call him first thing tomorrow to let him know what happened."

"Okay, be sure to call if you need me."

"You'll be the first one I call."

They walked into the foyer of the mansion and switched on the lights. It was a cheerful looking house and one would never realize the horror that had happened here today. Debra checked the boxes to see what she might need to bring tomorrow. It looked as though there were enough refreshments, sodas, brochures, and other paper work for the day, not that she was expecting anyone to show up. She checked Jett's visitor log and saw that she did have one looker, Elana Palmer. She wondered if it was just a curious neighbor or an authentic buyer. She hoped it was a buyer, a serious buyer, but wasn't holding her breath.

"Looks like everything I might need is here. I wonder if Jett put any stuff that I might need in her car?" she said to no one in particular.

"I'll take a look before the tow truck takes it away," Joe said as he hurried out the front door. The tow truck was coming up the driveway and Joe wanted to oversee the loading. Even though Jett was gone, he somehow thought he needed to protect her things.

"This box was in her car along with her purse and a few other personal items. I put her personal effects in your car."

"Thanks Joe, I'll take them to the office for her family."

Debra took one final look around the foyer before going outside and locking the front door. She didn't want to come back tomorrow but was obligated since Cory, the owner, was in town. She would call him first thing in the morning and hopefully he'd want to be there at the open house so she wouldn't be alone.

When the tow truck left with Jett's car, the guys were just finishing up with their clean-up. Debra hoped nothing showed through when the water dried but if it did, she could try to scrub it tomorrow before anyone showed up.

They all climbed into their cars and headed out the driveway. Debra left first then the deputies followed by Joe's car.

"Remember, call me if you need me," Joe called from his window.

"I will," Debra answered. She would have her assistant, Cindy, look at Jett's personnel file for information on Jett's next of kin and get that to the sheriff. She would call her tomorrow and have her go to the office to gather the information. She didn't think she would mind going in on Sunday under the circumstances. Cindy was one of the only friends Jett seemed to have and they weren't close.

Even though it was only a few miles to Debra's house, it seemed like a long, tiresome ride and Debra was tired but bug-eyed. She hoped she could sleep but knew she wouldn't. She'd have a glass of wine before turning in to try to help her sleep.

The next morning Debra awoke around six am and dragged herself out of bed to face the day. She showered, dressed in comfortable slacks, blouse and shoes and ate breakfast before calling Cory. She waited to call him until she was ready to leave her house for the mansion.

"Cory, sorry to bother you so early but I've got some terrible news. Jett had an accident at the property yesterday and has died. I'm going out for today's open house if you'd like to meet me there," she said to his voice mail. She was glad he didn't answer because she didn't want to go into the details of yesterday just yet.

Debra pulled into the driveway of LaBelle Mansion a few minutes before 9:00. She was skeptical about being here but knew she had to show up for the open house especially since the owner was in town and there was one name on Jett's list. If he hadn't have been visiting and in such a bad mood, she might have begged off but to protect the integrity of her company, she continued with the open house.

She parked her car a few feet away from the walkway and as she got near the steps, she noticed there was no evidence left of the horrible accident. Once she was satisfied with the appearance of the walkway and grass, she tried to avoid looking at the place where Jett had died. It felt somehow strange and foreboding to be here and she hoped a few people would stop to look at the property. She also hoped Cory would come out and stay for the open house. She didn't want to be here alone and she didn't want to call the sheriff to babysit her.

"Hello, this is Debra" she said after letting her phone ring several times.

"Hello Deb, Cory here," the man at the other end said. "What happened?"

"Oh, Cory, Jett tripped and fell into the boot scraper and cut her throat. When she didn't answer her phone, I had the sheriff drive out and he found her. She was already dead when he arrived."

"Oh my god, just one more reason I want rid of that place. I'm coming out to look things over. I should be there in about an hour."

Debra sighed in relief as she pressed the button to hang up. Instead of walking around the property, she sat in the swing on the front porch looking out at the driveway trying to will someone to drive in. While she was waiting for Cory, she called Cindy and told her about Jett's accident and asked her to go to the office and get Jett's family information for the sheriff.

"Cindy, as soon as you give the sheriff the information, call me back and I'll notify Jett's family."

"I can notify them if you want," Cindy said hoping Deb wouldn't take her up on the offer.

"Thanks but I think it best if I do it. After all, I am or was her employer."

Around 11:00 Cory drove up the driveway and parked beside Debra's car. When he got out, he had a bag with sandwiches and chips for their lunch. He walked up on the porch with a look of despair on his face. Debra could see he was worried about the recent events and it seemed he'd aged a few years overnight.

"Hi Deb, I brought some lunch for us. I'm going to stay this afternoon if you don't mind."

"That's the best news I've heard in a long time, you staying, not the lunch although lunch sounds pretty good too."

"So where's this boot scraper?" Cory asked. "I want to get rid of it."

"The sheriff took it in an evidence bag. I told him I didn't want it on the property so he bagged it and took it with him. If you want it, I'll have him bring it out."

"Hell no, I don't want it. He can keep it or toss it," Cory told her.

"I'll grab you a chair and a soda and we'll eat lunch. Hopefully someone will show up this afternoon," Debra told him.

"We have ham and swiss on rye or turkey breast with American cheese, which do you want?" Cory asked as he pulled the sandwiches out of the bag.

"I'll take the turkey and some of those chips," Debra said as she handed him a soda.

"Deb, I'm more serious than ever about lowering the price on this place. I'm prepared to offer it for $50,000 to the first person who drives up today. I talked to Jill this morning and she said to sell it for whatever we could get or give it away. Now with the tragedy last evening, I'm determined to get rid of it right now!"

Chapter 5

It was almost 1:30 when Elana and Scott turned into the driveway of LaBelle Mansion. Scott drove slowly looking at the grounds and trees on either side.

"These are nice but might take some upkeep so they don't get out of hand," he said looking at the trees. "But the grounds behind the trees look pretty good in a rustic sort of way. If we buy it, I can always hire a gardener to help with the outside."

As they got closer to the house, Elana noticed two cars and neither was Jett's. Her mind was racing as she tried to see who was on the porch. It appeared to be a man and a woman sitting in the chairs but she still couldn't see Jett.

"I wonder if Jett's here yet."

Scott pulled in to an open space beside the first car. He and Elana got out and slowly walked up the brick walk to the porch, looking around at the front yard. When they got to the steps, they went up to where the two were sitting.

The woman stood and offered her hand to Scott. "Hello, I'm Debra Baxter with Baxter Properties and this is Cory Jenkins, the owner of this fabulous property," she gushed. "I'm so glad you stopped by to see this beautiful home."

"Hi, I'm Scott Palmer and this is my wife Elana," Scott said as he shook first Debra's hand and then Cory's.

Elana looked around for Jett and before even saying hello asked, "Where's Jett?"

"Oh, did you know Jett?" Debra asked somewhat surprised.

"No, I was here yesterday and decided to come back today with my husband. Jett said she would be here both days."

"I'm sorry Elana, Jett passed away last evening," Debra said quietly.

"No way, what happened?"

"Well, you'll hear it soon enough," Debra started to explain. "She fell here and cut her throat and bled to death before anyone found her."

"Wow, that's awful. She seemed like such a nice lady. Where did she fall?" Elana asked for no particular reason.

"She fell down the steps," Cory offered. "She hit a boot scraper and it cut her throat. It was horrible."

"No shit, you know we were talking about how dangerous that thing would be if someone fell on it. Where's the scraper now?" Elana asked as she looked in the direction of where it should have been.

"The sheriff took it so no one else would get hurt," Debra told them.

"Can we still see the property today?" Elana asked.

"Most certainly, that's why we're here," Debra and Cory said simultaneously.

"We'll start with the mansion, then the smaller house, the carriage house and then the old school. Did Jett give you any information about the place?"

"Just that it was pretty old and the school building was a whore house during the Civil War and then was turned into a school. Oh, and she said it's rumored to be haunted, isn't that a hoot? Come on ghosties and show yourselves. I think every old house around has that reputation. People do like to make up stories."

"The place is quite old, the school was built in the late 1700s. The mansion and smaller house were both built just after the Civil War. The carriage house was built later as was the barn. There's a little over a hundred acres all fenced and mostly level," Cory offered solemnly wanting to get off the subject of ghosts. He didn't want to say there were ghosts or that there weren't.

"My wife and I remodeled and modernized the mansion after we bought it. It was in a sad state of repair with no running water or electricity."

"Why are you selling?" Scott asked.

"My wife and I have other interests and the place seems far too big for us in our later years. When my wife's mother took sick, we decided to move closer so we could care for her if necessary," Cory said as he crossed his fingers.

"Is it really haunted?" Elana joked.

"I've heard tales but I don't believe in such nonsense," Cory offered. "As you stated, I wouldn't be surprised if every house over 100 years old has some kind of haunting tale attached to it.

"Elana, you saw the mansion yesterday, do you want to look at it again today?" Scott asked.

"Not really, instead, let's look at the smaller house and the carriage house and if there's still time, try to go inside the old school. I'm really curious about the school building. I want to see how much work it might take to remodel it."

"I'll walk around it if we have time after looking at the rest of the property. If it suits you, I'm more than all right with it."

"Sounds good to me, I don't need to look at this house again if you're okay with not taking the tour," she told Scott.

"Let's start with the small house," Debra suggested. "From there we can go to the carriage house and finish up at the school."

"Cory, what's the history of this place?" Scott inquired as they walked to the small house.

"Well, the school building was originally built as a glebe house in the late 1700s. The stone was brought in from a quarry about ten miles from here. They say the pastor held services in one side of the building and lived in the other."

"Its most famous period, I'd have to say, was during the Civil War. It was a brothel that catered to both the Confederate and the Union soldiers. It's said that while they were on the property, they were to leave the war behind and I guess they did."

"After the war, the madam married a Confederate officer who built the mansion for her. He didn't want to run a brothel so they opened a school for young women. They educated the girls who worked in the brothel so they could find employment elsewhere. He built the small house for the couple that ran the school."

"I'm not sure when the carriage house was built but I'm told it was built by a wealthy couple who purchased the property. They ran the school for a while then the property went through several different owners before sitting vacant for many years."

"When we bought it, we completely remodeled the mansion, trying to bring it back to its original beauty along with modernization. Others had started remodeling but didn't finish the jobs. We were going to try to restore the school but that was going to be a pretty huge task and we aren't as young as we used to be," Cory explained, trying to make it sound as attractive as he could.

"Interesting history, what about the ghosts?" Elana asked with a snicker.

"Well, I don't know much about any ghosts but there's an old tale that one of the girls or farm hands at the brothel went crazy and tortured three men and then fed them to the hogs before they were dead," Cory laughed. "Maybe they're still pissed. I know I'd be upset if hogs ate me."

"Guess I'd come back and haunt someone if hogs ate me," Scott laughed.

There was a porch across the front of the small house and as Debra unlocked the door Elana caught a glimpse of something that looked like an old woman in a sunbonnet and a long dress. The woman was more of a mist than a person and seemed to be just beyond the porch. She batted her eyes a few times and it was gone so she thought it was just the way the sun was shining through the trees and forgot all about it.

They all followed Debra into the front room of the house. It was in need of some tender loving care and lots of remodeling. The room was across the front of the house and the hardwood on the floor was worn. The wall paper and woodwork were peeling but still the room felt cozy. There was a fireplace on one side and an old stair well on the back wall. A door at the bottom of the steps led to the kitchen. They looked around the room and then went upstairs before looking at the rest of the downstairs.

"Be careful on these steps," Debra warned. "They're steep and some might be rotten. I'm not sure how long it's been since anyone used these steps. Probably not since the school closed years ago."

At the top of the stairs, there was a small hallway with a door to each of the two small rooms. Overhead was what appeared to be a trapdoor to the attic. Both rooms were in the same condition as the front room but it appeared as though the structure was sound.

"There doesn't appear to be any signs of a leaking roof," Scott said as he looked around.

Each room had a small closet, a fireplace and two windows. After looking around upstairs, they all went back down the steps to look at the kitchen.

The kitchen was a small room with a porch on one side. It had a fireplace, an old sink with a pump and nothing more. The walls, woodwork and floors were in bad shape but not so bad that they couldn't be redone.

"Looks like this house will need plumbing, electricity and a lot of remodeling," Scott said to no one in particular.

"Yes, I don't think it's been lived in for years," Cory volunteered. "We thought about remodeling it for my mother-in-law but she got sick before we could do that."

"It is kind of quaint and cozy," Elana offered as she caught a glimpse of the old woman. This time, she seemed to be standing near the back door of the house. Once again Elana dismissed it as the sun or a shadow. After all, she didn't believe in ghosts and everything had a logical explanation.

"Okay, let's head over to the carriage house," Debra announced.

"I think I'll go over to the school and see where all we can safely go while you all tour the carriage house," Cory said. He didn't want to ever go into that building again.

"Fine, we won't be long," Debra said.

Debra, Scott and Elana walked down the walkway to the carriage house. Inside there was a garage along with three rooms and a loft. There was a ladder attached to one wall to get into the loft. One room was finished with paneling and hardwood flooring; the others weren't finished and appeared to have been used as storage. The garage portion looked like a typical garage.

As they walked into the finished room, Debra said, "This is where Cory's mother-in-law painted while she was visiting. She was becoming a well-known artist so Cory fixed this room up especially for her to use as a studio. The other rooms are pretty rough but have great potential. The only thing I wouldn't like is the garage being so far from the house, especially when it's raining or snowing."

"Yes, it is quite a ways from the house. If we bought it, I'd probably have a garage built closer to the house," Scott replied.

"This is beautiful, I could sit in here and study without any distractions," Elana told Scott.

"Go ahead and peek in the other rooms and the loft if you want," Debra told them. "I'll just wait outside."

They each peeked through the doors to the other rooms and Scott climbed the ladder and looked at the loft and then went to look at the garage.

"Looks good," Scott said, "this garage is huge with plenty of room for the classic car that I want to buy someday."

Elana cautiously looked around expecting to see the old lady again and was relieved when she didn't.

They left the carriage house and walked to the school where Cory was waiting on the porch.

"I think we can look at the whole building without any problems, just be careful where you step," Cory said to no one in particular.

As they stepped into the front room, Elana gasped, "That staircase is magnificent! Looks like something right out of a movie."

"It is quite beautiful even in its state of disrepair," Cory offered.

"The brothel was a large parlor across the front of the house over to the staircase. The original bar is still in back where I imagine it was in earlier times. In the back there are rooms that I'm told were used as hospital rooms during the Civil War. Confederates were treated on one side and Federals on the other," Cory said. "The kitchen and dining room were where the old church was located with a smaller room behind that I imagine was the pastor's study.

They walked around the downstairs and Elana took mental notes on how she could remodel. She especially wanted to keep the stairway and the bar.

Upstairs was a long hallway from one side of the building to the other. There were five rooms on each side of the hall each with a beautiful door with antique hardware to match. They looked in each room but didn't notice the rocking chair in one of the rooms had begun to slowly rock back and forth. Elana thought she heard a small, rhythmic creak coming from one of the rooms but dismissed it as just an old building settling.

"Oh my, it's almost 4:30," Debra exclaimed looking at her watch. "We should wrap this up unless you want to look at the mansion again. That shouldn't take along.

"Time flies when you're having fun," Elana said with a smile. "I think we're finished looking.

The walked back down stairs and took a quick look at the kitchen, dining room, and small room behind it and then went out to the porch.

Cory locked up the school building and they walked back over to the mansion. He tried to read what Elana and Scott were thinking and wondered if he should make the first move at a price. Elana and Scott were chattering between themselves but Cory couldn't make out what they were saying.

"Debra, Cory, we are most definitely interested," Scott announced much to Elana's surprise.

"Fantastic," Cory said. "Debra and I can work with you on everything. I want to sell as soon as possible so my wife and I can take a much needed vacation. So would you like to make an offer?"

"Well, you're asking $450,000 and you're anxious to sell. The place needs a lot of work and it's been on the market for around five years so will you consider $250,000?" Scott offered.

"Ouch, that's $200,000 less than I'm asking," Cory said, secretly smiling and doing a happy dance. "Let me call my wife."

He went to the other side of the porch and pretended to make a phone call. When he came back, he said, "she wasn't too happy but finally agreed if you sign the papers today."

"No problem," Scott said. "We can follow you to Debra's office if you want. It will take a few days for us to get the down payment together but that won't be an issue."

Cory held his hand out to Scott and then to Elana, "deal," he said as he took both their hands.

Debra locked the house and they followed her and Cory back to the Baxter Properties office. As they were backing from the parking space Elana once again saw the old woman and decided she had a resident ghost. She wasn't sure if she was glad or not but she really did want this property and the woman looked harmless enough. She decided she would call her friend Katie and ask her since she was always seeing spirits. If this spirit turned out to be nasty, she was sure Katie could help her get rid of it.

Chapter 6

At the Baxter Properties office, Scott and Elana signed the offer to buy and made an appointment with Debra and Cory to meet the following Friday to finalize the deal and set a date for closing. Because of Elana's trust fund and Scott's promotion, they would be able to pay cash. Since no one was living on the property, the transaction should be completed relatively quickly. It couldn't happen fast enough for Cory. He, too, saw the old woman but didn't dare mention it to anyone, not even Debra. He had disclosed that there were rumors of the place being haunted with Debra as a witness so he should be covered if there were any future ramifications. Right now, that was the least of his worries.

When Scott and Elana got up to leave, both Debra and Cory shook their hands and thanked them for the transaction. They left with a sense of satisfaction at getting the property for such a terrific price and getting out of the tiny apartment. Elana was chattering about what she planned to do once they got moved in and Scott was thinking about what he could do with the landscape and carriage house.

"The first thing I want to do is go shopping for furniture. Should we hire someone to clean the place or do you think we can do that ourselves? I'm going to eventually need a live-in housekeeper so should I start looking for one now?" Elana asked questions nonstop.

"Slow down, honey, we have lots of time. We can use the furniture we have now until you're finished with school and we can clean the place on the weekends. As for a housekeeper, we'll both pick her out," he said with a grin.

"Oh no, I'm picking the housekeeper, you devil. I'm just so excited. I'm not sure I'll be able to study for my exams," Elana said.

"As soon as you finish classes tomorrow, you need to go to the bank and start the ball rolling on getting your trust fund released. We have the cash for this but it will take all we have and I'm not comfortable being broke. I won't get paid until the end of the month and my bonus won't be given until the end of the quarter. Oh and stop by the attorney's office and have him do a title search just to be sure there aren't any liens on the property," Scott told her.

"I have one class in the morning and the rest in the late afternoon so I'll have plenty of time to take care of everything. Do you realize that since we got the property for such a low price that we will have more than enough to remodel, set up my couples retreat and take a vacation?" Elana excitedly told Scott.

"How much is in your trust fund?" Scott asked. He had never discussed this with Elana so he had no idea.

"I didn't know until a few days ago but it's a little over four million," she beamed. "That's more than I ever imagined was there."

"I didn't know I married a millionaire," Scott laughed as he hugged her. "I figured it might be a few thousand but not four million!"

"Uh-huh, so now I know you didn't marry me for my money," Elana giggled as she squeezed Scott's hand.

"I might just keep you for your money though," he laughed.

"Aw, you'll keep me for more than my money," she said as she moved her hand to his crotch.

"Stop that, you'll make me wreck!"

"Then hurry up and get home, I've got some celebrating to do. It isn't every day we buy a plantation and this plantation feels so right for some reason. Did you get that feeling, too?"

"Yeah, I did. Want to stop for something to eat?" Scott asked.

"No, we have the Chinese food to warm up and there's plenty of beer and wine."

They pulled into the parking space at their apartment and walked up the steps hand in hand. Scott unlocked the door and scooped Elana up and carried her over the doorstep kicking the door shut with his foot and instead of putting her down, he moved on to the bedroom.

"Now that's what I call a celebration," Elana said later as she snuggled close to Scott's sweaty, naked body.

They both crawled out of bed and walked barefoot to the bathroom. Scott turned on the shower and they both stepped in. They leisurely lathered each other with soap and made love once again before rinsing and wrapping each other in the huge towels Elana loved.

"Let's warm up that food and have some beer," Scott said as he walked into the kitchen. "I'm starved."

Elana put the food in microwave bowls and started the microwave while Scott got the beer and glasses. "Let's watch TV while we eat," Elana said as she carried napkins and silverware to the living room.

When the food was warm, she filled two plates and carried them into the living room and settled on the couch beside Scott.

"When do you start your new job?" Elana asked Scott.

"The first of the month, and I'll be out of town some. Will that be a problem with the new place and all?"

"Not at all, I'll be so busy I won't even notice you aren't there," Elana teased.

"Why don't you see if you can find a housekeeper right away to help out? Scott asked. "There's going to be a lot of work around here." He didn't let on but he was concerned about her being alone in such a remote place.

"I think I'll post an ad at the university and check with the employment office. The rooms above the kitchen would be perfect as a little apartment for a live-in house-keeper. Maybe a couple of college girls could live there and take turns helping out," Elana said.

"That might work; we can sure afford to hire a couple."

Elana and Scott tried to watch a movie while they ate but neither could focus, they were so elated about their new home. Finally, they decided to call it a night and headed for bed.

"Let's get some sleep, morning is going to be here before you know it," Elana said as she gave Scott a quick peck on the cheek.

The next morning, they both got up before the alarm sounded. Scott went into the bathroom for a shower while Elana went to the kitchen to start breakfast. They watched the local news while they ate bacon, eggs and toast. The first story was about Jett. They said it was an unfortunate accident and then told when and where she would be buried. Elana made note of the funeral home so she could send flowers.

"I still can't believe she fell on that boot scraper," Elana exclaimed. "We had talked about how dangerous that could be never dreaming something like this would actually happen. I feel just terrible."

"Well I'm glad the sheriff took it. I don't want anything like that around after we move in," Scott said grimly. "I wonder if anyone else ever fell on it. It had to have been there for a long time."

"I sure hope not, but we would probably never hear if they had. I think I'm going to do some investigating on the history of the place. I love history and I'm sure this place has some interesting tales to tell," Elana said as she cleared the table and put the dishes in the dishwasher.

"Good idea, I'll help when I can. I can do some Internet searches and you can go to the court house and library. I'm sure we can dig up lots of fascinating things. I'd like to know about the girl that fed the men to the hogs."

"Yeah, if we're going to live in a historic place, we should know the history. I wonder if anyone has registered it as a historical landmark." Elana muttered.

"I've got to run, see you this evening," Scott said as he grabbed his briefcase and headed out the door.

"Hey, wait a minute," Elana called to him.

"What?"

"You forgot something."

"What?"

She ran over to him, wrapped her arms around his neck and kissed him passionately.

"That's what you forgot," she said.

"Oops, guess I'm excited," he said sheepishly.

"You can make it up to me when you get home this evening," Elana said as she patted his backside.

He grinned and walked out the door to his car and Elana made her way to the bathroom to get ready for her first class.

Elana got to the school just in time for her class but knew she wasn't in the mood for a boring lecture.

Oh please, quit droning, Elana pleaded silently as the professor discussed his latest project that had nothing to do with Sociology. She hated this class but needed the credit and if a person showed up for class and didn't fall asleep they were assured at least a B.

When the class was over, she made a beeline for her car and headed to the bank. She had four hours before her next class and wanted to get things started with her trust fund and she wanted to stop by the attorney's and start a deed search on the property.

"I'd like to speak to Mr. Calhoun," Elana told the receptionist at the bank.

"Sure Elana, I'll tell him you're here. Have a seat."

"Thanks," Elana said as she took a seat in the waiting area. She looked around the waiting room and was impressed by how warm and inviting it felt. Most banks seemed cold and impersonal to her.

"Bill, Elana Palmer is here to see you," the receptionist said into the phone.

"Send her in," Bill Calhoun said. Bill was an old friend of the family and he had been expecting a visit from Elana since her trust fund was due to mature this week.

"Go on back, Elana," the receptionist motioned her towards the hallway.

"Hi Bill," Elana said as she entered the office and took a seat.

"I guess you're here to start the process for your trust fund. Your grandparents were certainly a generous couple."

"Yes they were. I found a terrific piece of real estate that Scott and I are going to buy and I need to get the money moved to my account."

"That's great, let me get the paperwork started and it should be taken care of in a couple of days or sooner. When's your birthday?"

"Tomorrow," Elana answered. "I thought I'd be sad to turn 30 but I'm ecstatic."

"Good for you, most really hate their 30th birthday more than any of the others."

"I'll have Scott stop in and sign the papers once everything is in order. I want him to be able to get to the money as well as myself."

"Okay, I'll just pull up the account and make the transfer to your account and have you sign the papers and we'll be all set. Scott can stop in whenever he has time, it'll only take a couple of minutes."

He entered the information into the computer, hit a button and the printer started. He reached into the print tray, took out the form, had Elana sign both copies and gave one to her.

"All done," he said. "It'll all be official tomorrow."

"Can I withdraw $250,000 later this week?" Elana asked.

"We can give you a cashier's check, not cash. Is that the down payment for the property?" he asked.

"No that's the total purchase price."

"Oh, where's this property?" Bill asked.

"It's the LaBelle Plantation out on Highway 2."

"And they are selling it for only $250,000? That's a steal. What's wrong with it?"

"The seller just wants to sell so he and his wife can move on."

"Isn't that where that real estate agent died a couple of days ago? Or did you know about that?" he asked reluctantly.

"Yes it is and I did know about it. I talked to her the day she died. It was quite a shock to go back on Sunday and hear the news. A terrible accident."

"And you still want to buy the place? I'm not sure I would."

"It's a beautiful house and the old school has lots of possibilities. I want to start a couples retreat when I graduate and the school building will be perfect. Scott and I can't wait to get out of our little apartment and into a home of our own and this is such a great opportunity for us," Elana explained. "It was an unfortunate accident but it doesn't mean we shouldn't buy a home we both fell in love with at first sight."

Bill smiled, stood up, and offered his hand to Elana.

"Thanks for taking care of things for me, Bill," she said as she shook his hand. "It means a lot to have a friend of the family to look out for my interests."

She left the bank and went to the attorney's office. The receptionist was on the phone and motioned for her to sit down. When she hung up, Elana told her she needed a title search for property she was about to buy so the receptionist took the information and told her it would take about 3 days and she would call when it was completed.

"There's a $150 fee for the title search payable today," the receptionist told Elana.

Elana took out her check book and wrote the check, got her receipt and left the office.

She still had plenty of time before her next class so she decided to do a deed search herself since the court house was just a block away. She walked up the steps, into the main entrance and looked at the directory. The sign said the county clerk's office was on the second floor so she walked up the stairs and found the clerk's office at the end of the hall.

She had never searched deeds before so she had to ask the clerk behind the counter where the deeds were and how to go about searching. The girl was eager to help her and stayed in the record room to be sure she was on the right track with her search. She started with the current owner, Cory Jenkins.

According to the deed, he and his wife purchased the property for $850,000.

My gosh, they're taking a $600,000 loss. Either they're super rich or super stupid or there's something terribly wrong with the place. What could possibly be wrong that we can't fix for that price though, Elana thought to herself. She wrote the information in a note pad she carried and proceeded to look for the prior owners. She was astonished at what she found. There seemed to be several previous owners and most didn't own the property for very long, especially after the school was closed down. She worked until she had just enough time to grab a sandwich and get to her class.

Chapter 7

When Elana got to her class, she knew she would have a difficult time concentrating on the lecture even though this was one of her favorite classes and the instructor was quite interesting. As soon as her finals were completed, she would have enough credits to graduate and eligible to start her internship and her PhD dissertation. She was required to work an internship before she could get her state license.

She had already been approved to intern with Dr. Meadows, a very popular and reputable psychologist. She would work three days a week in his office and two days a week shadowing him and other doctors at the hospital. She was going to start on her PhD this winter since she wants to have this credential as soon as possible. She feels this will greatly add to the success of her business.

It would be difficult juggling work, getting her new home ready, writing her dissertation, and setting up a business but she was up for the task even though it would be difficult.

The work wouldn't be too difficult since she was only observing, not dealing directly with patients but there would be periodic evaluations that she would need to prepare for. She was sure her evaluations would be above average.

I think if I can find two girls to help out for room and board I can have the place ready by the time I finish my internship, she thought to herself. *Just need to find someone who won't want to run around every evening and weekends. Surely there are a few girls that have more on their minds than partying and men.*

After her final class was over, Elana stopped by the student placement office to post an ad for a couple of girls to work for her and Scott. She wasn't sure how to interview and choose someone so she would probably work with Ms. Jacobs, the placement officer.

"Good afternoon, Ms. Jacobs," Elana said as she reached to shake Ms. Jacobs hand. "My husband and I are buying a plantation and will need a couple of girls to help out with housekeeping and such for room and board and I'm wondering if I can advertise through the placement office."

"Of course, when will you need them to start?" Ms. Jacobs asked as she turned to her computer.

"Probably by the end of the month. We won't close on the property until the end of next week and will move over the weekend. There are two rooms with baths that are separate from the rest of the house where they can live in privacy. I want someone who can help evenings and weekends with keeping the house and helping us with odd jobs, nothing heavy though," Elana replied. "Hopefully there are a couple of girls who are more interested in securing a place to stay than they are in partying and men."

"I'm sure there are," Ms. Jacobs smiled. "Will there be any pay or just room and board?"

"Well, I can afford to pay some but I was thinking more in terms of room and board. What do you think?"

"Room and board is certainly attractive considering the cost of apartments and food so let's see what we can do. If we don't find any applicants we can always offer some pay. I'll prepare an ad and email it to you for approval. We can post it on the school web site, the bulletin boards and the local paper. There's no charge for this service but we do accept donations if the positions are filled."

"Great, I'll watch for the email, I'm anxious to move on this and the sooner the better," Elana told her as she walked towards the door.

"I'll have the email to you this evening," Ms. Jacobs said as she turned to her computer.

Elana walked down the steps and across the campus lawn to the parking lot. She had a spring in her step and was thrilled to be moving closer to her dream. She wanted to spend her time planning her next moves but knew she had to study for her exams. She couldn't chance failing any of her courses now that she was so close to her perfect future.

She stopped at the market and picked up a couple of steaks, salad mix, dessert, and wine for dinner. When Scott got home, they could grill the steaks on the grill they kept on the small balcony. Elana would study while waiting for Scott and then hit the books again after they ate.

Scott got home about an hour after Elana and was eager to get the steaks started. He had an important meeting with corporate directors and had missed lunch even though they did provide donuts and coffee. He hoped this wouldn't be the norm because he was a bit of a health fanatic and could see himself losing his ripped physique if he started skipping lunch for donuts.

"These are good looking steaks," he smiled at Elana. "Do you want yours medium like always?"

"Yep, crisp on the outside and bloody on the inside. I'll make a salad while you grill," she said as she handed him a glass of wine.

"How was your day?" Elana asked as she chopped the vegetables into a bowl.

"Horrible, meetings all day with no real lunch. Oh and I have to be out of town most of next week. When did Debra say we were meeting to close?"

"Next Friday. Will you be back by then?"

"Yeah, I fly back to town on Thursday so I can take Friday off."

"Where are you going?" Elana asked.

"The San Francisco office and I'll need to make sure my passport is in order because in three weeks I'll be flying to the office in the Cayman Islands."

"How long will you be there?"

"Three or four days at least," Scott called in from the balcony.

"So who's going to help me move? I doubt I can do it by myself."

"I asked Bill and Al if they could give us a hand and they should be available anytime we need them. Both are out of work right now."

"What's the charge, two or four six-packs?" Elana laughed.

"Probably six or eight if I know Bill and Al. Steaks are done, where's the plates?"

"Right here," Elana said as she carried two plates out to the balcony. "Yum, these look delicious."

Elana put the plates on the coffee table in front of the couch along with the salad and wine. Scott started a movie while Elana poured the wine and put salad into small bowls for each of them.

"Is this movie OK?" Scott asked.

"Perfect, I love horror movies about houses," Elana said as she crinkled her nose.

"Aw, you're not scared are you? I can find something else."

"Oh no, these old movies are kind of funny after you watch for a while," Elana said but she wasn't too sure she meant it. She really didn't want to watch a movie when she should be studying but she didn't want to disappoint Scott.

"Let's eat and then we can relax for a bit before bedtime," Scott said as he cut his steak.

"I have to study for exams, no relaxing for me until after I take my last test," Elana pouted.

"Need any help?" Scott asked.

Elana shook her head no since she preferred to study in her own way without any interruptions.

"O-o-o-o, you made this perfect," Elana sighed as she bit into her steak. "I might let you cook all the time."

"Well if you buy steaks like these, I'll take the job."

They ate as they watched the opening scenes of the movie. It was about an old house that was haunted by a previous owner and his wife. They waited until the young couple who lived there were fast asleep and then moved various pieces of furniture and other items.

"This movie is so lame," Elana laughed as she watched the old man move a kitchen chair from the table to other side of the room.

"It is isn't it," Scott chuckled as he watched.

Just then the old man in the movie found the butcher knife and gave his wife a wicked grin. "Let's have some fun," he said, his wicked grin getting wider.

They crept up the stairs to the room where the couple was sleeping, creaked open the door and stood at the foot of the bed waiting for the couple to wake. When they woke a few seconds later, they saw the old man holding the butcher knife in the air as if he were going to stab them.

The young wife screamed and the husband cursed as they watched the old man and woman slowly disappear and the knife fall to the floor with a clatter.

"If it's OK with you, I'm going to go study," Elana told Scott. She was feeling uneasy watching this movie even though it was lame.

"Go ahead, I'm going to get my things ready for tomorrow and then going to shower and get to bed."

Elana gave him a quick hug and peck on the cheek and went to her computer and was soon engrossed in her studies.

It was after two when she finally turned off the computer and went to bed. Scott was fast asleep and softly snoring. She watched him sleeping for a while and then turned off her bed lamp and snuggled close to him and promptly fell asleep.

Scott was up at six the next morning and tried to be quiet so he wouldn't awaken Elana. She didn't wake until eight or so. Scott left a note saying not to wait dinner since he would be late. That was all right with Elana because she wanted to study and didn't want to be disturbed. She was so close to finishing her studies and certainly didn't want to mess up on any of the exams.

Elana's first exam was in the morning and the others were in the afternoon. She had contacted the lawyer to do a property search just to be sure there were no liens on the property and it was to be ready today. She would stop by after lunch and then stop by the bank to tie up loose ends with plenty of time to make it to her first afternoon class.

The first exam was relatively easy so Elana was sure she aced it but she was concerned about the ones this afternoon. She knew they would be more comprehensive and she would have to concentrate if she was going to make a decent grade.

I wonder if we are moving too fast on this house purchase, she thought to herself. *I just don't know if we will have time to get everything done that needs done.*

She wasn't having second thoughts, they were both just so busy right now and she didn't want to forget anything or screw up the deal.

"Hi Elana," Melanie, the receptionist at the lawyers office said. "Bill will be with you in a few minutes."

"Okay, thanks, I'll just sit and study while I wait," Elana said as she sat down and opened one of her books.

After about 15minutes, Bill opened his office door and motioned Elana in.

"Good afternoon, Elana," he said. "The property looks fine. I searched back five owners and none had a lien. The current owner has owned the property for six years. Before they bought it, it was owned by several others but none kept it very long. It sat vacant for several years before the current owner bought it. Do you want me to search back any further? You said the current owner is selling thousands of dollars below the asking price, can I ask why?" Bill inquired.

"No, no need to search back any further. The current owner says they don't need the money and they just want to be rid of it and move on. I think he thinks it's haunted," Elana laughed.

"Did he say that?"

"Not in so many words but I'm not worried about such silliness," Elana said. "Every old house is said to have a ghost so I'm not worried at all. Might be fun to have a ghost if it is true."

"So when are you taking possession and moving in?"

"We close next Friday and will move in as soon as possible. I want to get started remodeling the old school building so it will be ready to open when I finish my internship."

"Well, I wish you the best of luck and let me know if I can be of any assistance" Bill said as he handed Elana the paperwork and stood to show her out.

"Thanks, Bill," Elana said as she took the search documents and shook Bill's hand.

When she stopped by the bank, she was told everything was in order and that Scott had been by and signed the papers. She assured Mr. Calhoun that she and Scott would be stopping by to discuss investment options at a later date.

She checked her watch and saw she had enough time to stop by the convenience store for a cup of coffee and a snack to take back to class.

Chapter 8

When Cory arrived home Jill was waiting for him with a martini and a smile. "I'm so glad you unloaded that property," she said as she handed him his drink. "I want to celebrate."

"I have mixed feelings, what if something happens to those kids who are buying it?"

"Nothing is going to happen to them and we can't worry about that," she said as she sipped her drink. "They're adults and maybe whatever's there won't bother them like it did Mom. I wish I knew what happened that day. It was such a beautiful place and I never once thought about anything so horrific happening."

"I doubt we'll ever know what happened but it must have been horrific. I can't understand why nothing ever bothered us. Were you ever frightened there when you stayed alone or even when I was there?"

"Never. I always felt so happy and relaxed there that I honestly hated to leave but I knew Mom would never come back so I decided we should move on."

"I wonder if any of the other owners had problems," Cory said as he made himself another martini. "We close next Friday but if it's OK with you, I'm going to let Debra give the keys to the Palmers so they can start moving in if they want."

"Fine with me, I don't want anything more to do with the place even if we never get our money from them."

"We'll get our money, they are so enthused and I think this is their first home. I just hope they aren't making a mistake. I couldn't forgive myself if anything happened to that couple. I'd rather let the place sit and rot away first. I know I shouldn't worry but I can't help it."

"As I said, it's none of our affairs now, they're adults and if they don't like the place, they can sell. We can't worry about what we have no control over," Jill said. "I just remember the day Mom died. I'll never forget the phone call from Dr. Thomas the night before and the day that followed. I just hope in time, I can forget about all this and remember Mom as the happy, vital artist that she was, and not the frail old woman she became that night."

***

"Jill, this is Dr. Thomas and I'm afraid I have some bad news. Your Mother's worse and you should come right away."

"Oh dear, we'll be right there," Jill said as she put the receiver back in the cradle. "Mom's worse, we have to go over to the center right away."

"I'll get the car," Cory said soberly. He ran to the garage and drove the car up to the front of the house where Jill was waiting.

When they arrived at JoAnne's room, she was hysterical. She was waving her arms and crying out, "leave me alone, leave me alone."

"Mom, Mom, settle down, we're here with you," Jill said as she tried to comfort her Mother.

JoAnne looked at her daughter with hollow eyes that had a look of fear so terrifying that it frightened Jill.

"Mom, what's wrong?" Jill pleaded.

"They're back and they're trying to kill me."

"Who's back?" Jill questioned.

"The men, the men, they're back and they're trying to kill me."

"What men," Cory asked.

"The men from the carriage house," JoAnne cried. "They've come to finish the job."

"Mom, I don't see anyone," Jill said as she rocked her Mother in her arms.

"Oh they're here, they're just hiding, they'll show themselves soon."

Just then a nurse came in with a sedative for JoAnne. As soon as she injected her, she settled into a peaceful sleep.

"She must have had a terrible nightmare. What do you think she meant by the men from the carriage house. I've never seen any men anywhere near the carriage house," Jill said to Cory.

"I have no idea. I haven't seen any men anywhere on the property except for guests and none of them would harm her. Maybe someone was there while we were gone the night she..." Cory trailed off before saying she went crazy.

"We have to find out what happened that night but I'm afraid it will make her worse to ask. Maybe we should talk with the doctor to see if he thinks it's alright to question her," Jill said.

"At this point, I don't see what it will hurt. She's terrified and maybe talking will help. When she wakes up, we'll both talk to her."

"Why don't you go get something to eat and bring me back a pizza or a sandwich, I'm going to stay with her tonight," Jill told Cory.

"Alright, I'll be back later. I'm going to go home after you eat something and come back in the morning. I have some work to catch up on and this might be a long drawn out ordeal," Cory said as he left Jill with her mother.

About an hour and a half later Cory returned with a tuna on rye sandwich, French fries and hot coffee for Jill. She ate part of the sandwich and fries and drank the coffee, then held onto Cory's hand and stared down at her mother.

"I can't believe that such a short time ago she was a vibrant, healthy woman and now she is so old and frail," Jill said through tears.

"I know, she was the youngest seventy year old I knew. It looks as though she might sleep the night so I should be leaving now, I'll be back in the morning," Cory said as he kissed Jill on the cheek and wiped away some of her tears.

"I'll call you if anything changes. Drive carefully."

"I'll give you a call around midnight to see how she is," Cory said as he walked out the door.

Jill sat down in the chair beside her mother and looked at the frail old woman and wondered what had happened to do this to her mother. Something terrible must have happened while they were gone. She wished they hadn't left her alone and that they hadn't stayed out so long after dark.

Right at midnight, Cory called but there was no change. JoAnne was still sleeping peacefully and one of the nurses had brought Jill a pillow and blanket so she could try to get some sleep too.

"Call me if anything changes or first thing in the morning," Cory instructed. "Love you."

"Love you too, night," Jill said as she blew a kiss into the phone.

JoAnne slept fitfully through the night and woke around 7 the next morning.

"What are you doing here?" she asked when she saw Jill sitting in the chair beside her bed.

"You had a bad nightmare and the nurse called me in. How are you this morning?"

"I'm hungry as a bear, where's breakfast?"

"It'll be here in a few minutes. So do you remember your nightmare?" Jill questioned.

"Nope, and I don't want to," JoAnne insisted. "You can go on home after you eat some breakfast with me."

"Are you sure? I can stay with you if you want."

"I'm old, I'm not a child, and besides, I have things to do," JoAnne said firmly. "Now go on home as soon as we eat."

"Okay, if that's what you want. What are you going to do?"

"Nothing that you need to worry about."

"Here's breakfast," Jill said as the aide brought in both trays.

"Looks delicious," JoAnne said as she took the covers off her bacon, eggs, potatoes and toast. "And the coffee smells divine."

"It does look good and I can sure use some coffee," Jill told her mother trying to be upbeat.

When they finished breakfast, JoAnne lay back on her pillow and closed her eyes. She had a smile on her face and Jill wondered what she might be thinking.

For a split second, Jill thought she saw three shadows floating above her mother's bed.

Just then her mother opened her eyes, shook her fist and screamed, "You're not getting me, now leave. No, no, leave her alone and I'll go with you."

Somewhere, from far, far away, Jill imagined she heard laughter, evil laughter. She looked at her mother and saw her sightless eyes wide with fear and her mouth contorted into a silent scream.

"Mom," Jill said as she took her mother's hand. Then she screamed because it was evident her mother was dead. "Someone help me!" Nurses came running into the room and confirmed Jill's fears.

"Cory," Jill screamed into the phone, "Mom died! She ate her breakfast and laid back and died. Please come as quick as you can!"

"I'll be right there," Cory told her hoping she wouldn't go into hysterics.

When Cory arrived, Jill was still sitting in the chair beside the bed that had earlier held her mother. Nurses had stripped the bed and packed up JoAnne's belongings but Jill wouldn't leave until Cory got there.

"Oh Cory, it was terrible. I thought she was having another nightmare. If I'd known she was dying, I could have held her hand, told her I loved her or something. I didn't tell her I loved her. Oh Cory, what am I going to do?"

"We'll get through this and then we'll take a long holiday," Cory soothed her.

"That would be nice. I need to just get away. After the funeral, let's go to Italy or Greece and relax for a month or so."

"That's a wonderful idea. We do need to get away for a while."

Jill didn't tell Cory about the shadows or the laughter. She was too frightened to speak the words.

Who was Mom talking to when she died, she wondered to herself. She trembled when she thought about her mother's last words.

Chapter 9

Cory called Debra early Tuesday morning and explained they would have to postpone closing but didn't feel he needed to explain the reason.

"Jill and I can't make it down Friday so can we reschedule the closing?"

"Elana and her husband will be disappointed but I'll call and ask," Debra said a little disappointed herself.

"Tell them they can have the keys today if that will ease their minds."

"That might help. I'll call and see."

"Elana, Debra here," Debra said when Elana answered her phone.

"I'm afraid we are going to have to reschedule the closing."

"Oh no, we were looking forward to looking the property over this weekend and moving in right away."

"Well, Cory has agreed to go ahead and give you the keys so it will be all right to move in as planned as long as everything is to your satisfaction."

"That's wonderful. I'll check with Scott about his schedule. Will we still be able to close if he has to sign the papers later?"

"I don't see why not, everything else is in order and this is a cash sale."

"Great, if it's all right, I'd like to stop by today and pick up the keys then. I'll be right by your office."

"I'll have them ready," Debra said smiling to herself. She hoped giving them the keys before closing the sale was a good idea but this was Cory's wishes.

Things were moving so fast that Elana hardly had time to think but she was excited and now she planned to take her time looking at their new purchase. She hoped Scott would be able to go with her when she toured their new home but if he couldn't, maybe she could get her best friend, Megan, to go with her. If no one was available, she would enjoy the tour by herself.

Elana stopped by the real estate office on her way home and chatted with Debra for a few minutes. It felt so good to have the keys to her new home in her hand.

"I can't wait to do another tour, a really slow tour of the place. If Scott can't go with me, I'll get my friend to go along. She should be free one afternoon this week. She has been beside herself wanting to see the place."

"I would take someone with me to do the tour, it's more fun that way," Debra said thinking there was no way she would go to that place alone unless she just had to. She wasn't sure why she was so uncomfortable at this property. She had never felt uneasy at any of her other listings.

"I'm anxious to show it off and really anxious to get settled in. This is our first home and it is going to be so special. I can just see my practice growing after I get all set up," Elana beamed.

"I'm sure it will," Debra replied.

Elana stopped and bought a pizza and sodas for dinner. She would buy some steaks and all the fixings tomorrow but tonight, she didn't feel up to making a large meal.

"I'm home," Scott called as he walked through the front door.

"In the kitchen, cooking up a storm," Elana called.

"Yeah, I'll bet you are, I smell pizza."

"Yep, pizza and I made a salad so get washed up while I set the table and get the drinks."

"Yum, I'm so hungry I'd eat cardboard if you put tomato sauce and pepperoni on it," Scott laughed as he washed his hands and face.

"Guess what, we got the keys to the property today."

"Why, we aren't closing until Friday."

"The Jenkins have to postpone closing so they decided to go ahead and give us the keys so we could look the place over and start moving in if we wanted to."

"Sounds good, maybe we can go out this weekend and get our bearings and see what we need," Scott replied.

"I would love to."

"Oh, my boss, Stan wants you to have lunch with us tomorrow. Can you make it around 12:30?"

"Sure, what restaurant?"

"The Blue Goose on 67th Street. There's parking in the rear."

"Swanky, I'll definitely be there. What should I wear?"

"No need to dress up, just some nice jeans and top would be fine."

"Wonder why he wants me to have lunch with you all?" Elana questioned.

"He said something about one of his relatives who used to live on the plantation and he wanted to talk to us about her."

"Now that is interesting. Wonder how long ago she lived there."

"I think during the Civil War but not sure."

"Oh if that's so, maybe she was the madam," Elana laughed. "Or one of the girls."

"Guess we'll find out tomorrow. Now let's eat. I want to watch some TV and then hit the bed. I have to be at work by seven in the morning."

Elana walked into the Blue Goose at exactly 12:30. The hostess met her, asked her name and escorted her to the table where Scott and Stan were already seated.

"I hope I'm not late," Elana apologized.

"Oh no, not at all," Stan said as he stood and extended his hand to Elana. "I'm Stan Reynolds and I'm sure you know Scott here," he said with an infectious laugh.

102

"How do you do, Mr. Reynolds, and yes, I sure do know Scott."

"Call me Stan, everyone else does."

"Okay, Stan it is," Elana said as the hostess seated her.

"Honey, we've already ordered and I ordered you tuna on rye with fries and iced tea. I hope that's all right," Scott told Elana.

"Perfect, thanks for ordering for me."

"Elana, Scott tells me you all bought LaBelle plantation."

"Oh yes, and I'm so excited."

"Small world, my great, great, great, grandmother lived there during the Civil War."

"How fascinating, was she the owner?" Elana inquired.

"No, but she did work there," Stan replied.

Elana wasn't sure how to respond since she knew the place was a brothel and she didn't want to embarrass Stan by asking the wrong questions. He might be embarrassed if his ancestor was a lady of the evening.

"Actually, she worked for the owner. I believe the owner's name was Belle something or other. Belle's place was a brothel. My grandmother was a mulatto named Lucy and she was one of Belle's 'girls'. When the war ended, Lucy married Sam Reynolds, the bartender. Sam was a white man so the marriage was looked down upon by most everyone."

"The brothel was turned into a school for young women and the big house was built for Belle and her new husband and the small house was built for Lucy and

Sam. That's pretty much all I know but hope someday to learn a whole lot more. Anyway, Lucy's journal has been passed down to me but I've never gotten around to reading it and wonder if you'd like to borrow it."

"Oh my goodness, I'd love to borrow it to read," Elana said excitedly. "There's no telling what information it might contain about the property. I want to learn all I can about the history of the place."

"Its old, faded and the writing is difficult to read but I brought it with me just in case you wanted it," Stan said as he laid a box on the table.

"Oh, I don't know what to say except thank you!"

"Keep it as long as you want and after you've read it, you can tell me what it says."

"Oh I will, I will!" Elana exclaimed.

"Lunch is here so we better eat, Scott and I have a full afternoon," Stan said as the waiter placed their food in front of them.

"Can I get you anything else?" the waiter inquired.

"No, I think we're fine for now but in a few minutes, I'll need the check," Stan told him.

"Looks delicious," Scott said as he bit into his burger. Scott never turned down a cheeseburger with the works but he now had to forget onions.

"Elana, I hope you don't mind but we'll be taking Scott out of town quite a bit for a while. We have a lot of areas he will need to become familiar with in a short time," Stan said.

"I was hoping he wouldn't have to be away too much now that we've bought the property but I understand and am perfectly fine with it. I'm going to be busy myself with decorating the house, my internship and planning for my future business."

"Yes, Scott was telling me about your plans for a couples retreat. That's a fascinating idea and I'm sure you'll be quite a success."

After they ate, Scott kissed Elana on the cheek and told her he'd be home a bit late.

"It was so nice meeting you Elana and enjoy the journal," Stan said as he left with Scott.

"Nice meeting you too Stan and I will definitely enjoy the journal."

Elana gathered up the box with the journal along with her purse and made her way out of the restaurant. She was anxious to get home to start reading. Since Scott was going to be late, they would probably just have sandwiches and a salad for dinner so she could spend all evening pouring over the journal.

When she got to the apartment, she curled up on the sofa and took the journal out of the box. It felt so fragile, she was afraid of damaging it so she carefully opened the cover. The pages weren't as brittle as she was worried they might be. On the second or third page she saw the words: *Lucy Taylor born May 17 1846*.

She flipped through the journal and saw pages were indeed worn. The writing was faded and the words were going to be very difficult to read. She was determined to work at it because she was so curious about her new home and wanted to know about the people who lived there. As she was flipping through the pages, she came upon some very old photographs. One was of a young couple. The girl was beautiful and darker than the man so Elana assumed this must be Lucy and Sam. Another was of a dark skinned couple and another was of an elegant looking woman and man that Elana decided must be Belle and her husband. Another picture was of an elderly black woman. She looked a long time at the picture of the elderly black woman wondering why she seemed so familiar. She would make a note to ask Stan about these pictures.

"I might not get much sleep until I finish reading your journal, Lucy," Elana said to no one in particular. "I wish I could have met you and talked to you in person."

Just then the phone rang. "Elana, I have to go to Boston tomorrow so I won't be able to go with you on the tour of the property," Scott said somewhat disappointed. "Do you think you can get Megan to go with you? I don't feel comfortable with you going by yourself just yet."

"Oh darn, I was looking forward to looking at it with you but I'll call Megan and see if she's free. If she can't go, maybe Bill or Al will be available but I don't have any qualms about going by myself."

"No, I don't want you going by yourself until we get moved in. We don't know anything about the place and there might be who knows what there just waiting for an accident."

"OK, I'll make sure someone goes with me. What time are you leaving tomorrow?"

"Around ten. We fly out at 1:00 and will be back Tuesday afternoon."

"Do you want me to pack for you?"

"No, I'll toss some things in the suitcase when I get home. I'll be there in about an hour."

"See you then, oh, tell Stan I found some pictures in the journal and it looks like one might be his grandparents."

"I will, he'll be pretty excited if he hasn't already seen them. See you in a bit. Love you."

"Love you too."

As soon as she hung up, she dialed Megan's number.

"Hey Megan, Elana here, how would you like an adventure tomorrow?"

"What's up?" Megan asked.

"I'm going to tour my new property and Scott will be in Boston so I wondered if you'd like to go with me. We can grab some lunch a fabulous sea food restaurant near the property and then take the grand tour."

"I'm in if you're buying."

"Fantastic, pick you up around 10:30. Wear old clothes and comfortable shoes."

"Will do, see you tomorrow, bye."

OK, that's settled so now I can get back to the journal, Elana thought with a smile as she laid down the phone and picked up the journal. She was anxious to show the property to Megan and tell her all about the journal.

Chapter 10

Elana was fascinated by what she was reading. It was evident that Lucy had very little education and the pages were faded and difficult to read but she couldn't put the book down. It was like she was back in the 1800s living the life of a poor slave girl except it appeared Lucy wasn't a slave.

Luke, Mazy's man give me dis book to rite in for my birthday yesterday. I come to Bells to live cause I don't have no place else to go. Miz Bells a nice lady and Mazy like her.

Miz Bell say it time for me to earn my keep so I can work the kitchen the fields or the house. Mazy wants me to work the kitchen cause the fields too hard and the house is bad. I want to work the house cause the girls dress so purty look like they be so happy.

Elana kept reading and was amazed at what this young girl had to say.

I burned the biskits this mornin and Mazy hit me and told me to be more careful. I cried when she wasn't lookin. I don't like to git hit. She said Miz Bell would do worse than that when she found out and I was afeard that she might take a switch or belt to me.

When Miz Bell found out, she jest hugged me and said that acdents happen and I could see Mazy was real mad.

I talked to one of the girls bout workin the house and she said it weren't so bad. Jest had to take care of the men. I tol her I knew all about that cause even though he was my pappy Masta Taylor took me to his bed since I was 10. If I didn't do what he wanted he would whip me with his belt til I did.

The girls said I neednt worry bout gettin whipped at Bells cause Bell took care of the girls. Once a man beat a girl and Bell shot him clean tween the eyes and Luke and Sam carried him out and fed him to the hogs. When the sheriff come lookin no one said nothin.

I tol Bell I wanted to work the house stead of the kitchen. She said I could if it was al right with Mazy but I said I dint need to ask Mazy. She said I would get paid half what the men paid for me along with my room and food. Then she tol me what I was to do. I tol

110

her bout Masta Taylor so she dint seem worried bout me bein too young to be wit men. Mazy be real upset and call me a hore but I dint care. She dint know I done knew men but I tell her in time bout Masta Taylor.

Mazy wont talk to me no more. She be real mad Mazy always seem mad ta. She worry to much bout me jest caus I her sister

Elana couldn't put the book down even though her eyes burned from trying to read the faded writing. She couldn't wait until Scott got home so she could tell him what she had already read. She felt so sorry for Lucy but was also amazed by her. She was mature well beyond her years.

Scott walked in the door and dropped his briefcase just inside the door. He looked beat but had a huge smile on his face.

"Hey beautiful, what's for dinner? I'm famished and in a terrific mood. When my orientation is completed, I will get a huge bonus and another raise."

"That's awesome, we're having sandwiches and salad. I sort of got caught up reading this journal and didn't think to cook. It is so fascinating, I wonder why Stan didn't read it."

Elana went into the kitchen a started to prepare sandwiches while Scott went to wash up. He came back just as Elana was carrying the sandwiches and salad to the living room.

"Tell me about it," Scott said as he settled onto the couch and starting eating. "Stan has told me a little about his grandmother but not much."

"Stan's grandmother was one of the girls in the brothel and she was the illegitimate child of her slave master. And he started having his way with her when she was ten even though she was his daughter. Pretty sick huh? I've only read about thirty pages and it's so interesting to see how people lived back then. They must have had a hard life."

"I'll have to fill Stan in tomorrow on the way to Boston. He was hoping you would be interested enough and able to read the journal. He tried but could only read a couple of pages because it was so faded and the writing didn't seem to make any sense to him."

"I know what he means, it's very difficult to read and she wasn't educated so I have to guess at some of the words. Want to watch a movie before we go to bed?" Elana asked.

"Yeah, that might be good. I need to relax a bit. It's been a bear of a week and there's no letup in sight. After we get back from Boston, we'll be flying to the Caymans for a few days. After that, I don't know. I'm really sorry I'm leaving you with so much to do but I don't have much choice."

"I understand and we're going to take this slow and easy. I can get us moved in and then we can just relax and take it one day at a time. It's not like we have a lot of furniture and the house is in excellent shape."

"Honey, you're something else. How did I get so lucky? Understanding, cute, sexy and a millionaire to boot. What more could a man ask for?" Scott teased as he leaned over and kissed her.

"Aw, you're just after my body and money."

"You bet," he said as he wrestled her to the couch. "Forget the movie, let's make our own fun then I'll pack."

While Scott was getting ready the next morning, Elana called Megan.

"Hey Meg, you still up for going on the house tour with me?"

"Wouldn't miss it," Megan replied. "Just have a couple of errands to run first but I'll be ready around 10:30. Meet you in front of my apartment."

"See you then."

Elana showered and dressed in jeans, tee shirt and sneakers then sat down to read some more in the journal. There were several pages that were so faded she couldn't make out the words. Maybe after she had gone through the whole book she might come back to the pages with a magnifying glass and better lighting to try to read them again.

Mazy Luke and Miz Bell left to visit Bell's sister in Tenesee. They be gone for a week and the saloon and house be closed while they gone. Us girls have orders to clean the house from top to bottom inside and out. wish I be goin wit them.

I glad we close the saloon but not sure I like all the cleanin

There talk of a war and everone scared. We ain't never been in a war. Word is it to free slaves. That be good but Miz Bell dont have no slaves so maybe it wont hurt us. She has 4 colored people workin for her but they be same as family but folks call dem slaves anyway.

Elana glanced at the clock and saw it was almost time to pick up Megan so she grabbed her purse and keys and headed out the door. Even though she would have loved to keep reading, she was just as anxious to take a good look at the property.

She pulled up to the curb where Megan was standing and waved her in.

"Been waiting long?" she asked.

"Nope, just came down." Megan was about 5'6" tall, slender with dark auburn hair pulled back into a pony-tail. She looked more like a teenager than a 29 year old woman in her jeans and tank top. She wore just a touch of lipstick and a bit of eye liner.

"The restaurant isn't far from the property. I'm famished and Chips and Chowder makes the best clam chowder I've ever eaten. Hope you're hungry."

"Chips and Chowder, I know that place. Darren used to take me there but we haven't been in over a year." Darren was Megan's live-in boyfriend. They used to have really good salmon cakes too."

"Well, let's get started so we can devour some of that seafood and then take the grand tour. Hope you're ready to be amazed."

"Ready. Are you going to need any help out there?" Megan told Elana.

"Oh my goodness, I'm going to need so much help and you can stay over if you want. There's plenty of room. I'm going to do my internship starting the first of the month and Scott is going to be traveling for almost forever it seems. Are you doing your internship too?"

"Yes, I'm going to work with Dr. Meadows starting the first of the month."

"Get out of town, that's where I'm interning. We can ride together," Elana squealed. "You know, once my internship is over and I have the place fixed up I'm starting a marriage counseling practice and a couples retreat. Maybe we could partner up. What do you think?"

"That would be awesome. I'll think about it and talk to Darren and let you know. Oh, this is so exciting!" Megan beamed.

"There's the restaurant. We can talk this over while we eat but no rush. I won't be ready to do much for several months."

They walked into the restaurant, were seated and gave the waitress their order. While waiting, they wandered around looking at pictures and other decorations. Elana noticed a picture of the old school house on her property and showed it to Megan.

"This must have been taken a 100 years ago. Look at how nice and neat everything looks. You can't see the mansion but it's behind the school."

"That place is beautiful. Does it still look like that?" Megan asked.

"No, it's in pretty bad repair but I think I can get it back to that look with some work."

Just then an old man walked up and asked, "Do you girls know the LaBelle planation?"

"Not really but this building is spectacular," Elana remarked.

"Quite a history, that place," the man said.

"Oh, tell us," Elana inquired. "We love to hear stories about old houses."

"Well to start, it's haunted. Bad things happen out there. Why just a while back a woman was murdered," he said seriously.

"What," Elana exclaimed. "When and what happened?"

"They say she fell on a boot scraper but I know better. It was those ghosts what killed her. Mark my word, bad things happens out there," he cackled.

"Have you seen the ghosts," Elana prodded.

"Don't have to. Lots of people will tell you the same thing. Just ask," he said in all seriousness.

"Thanks for the information sir," Elana said as she started back to the table. "Foods here."

116

"Wow, that old man spooked me," Megan said. "What did he mean about a woman being murdered there? That's pretty intense and scary if you ask me."

"The real estate agent that showed me the house did trip and fall on the boot scraper. When she hit it, she cut her carotid artery and bled to death but she certainly wasn't murdered by ghosts. Cripes, that's how rumors get started," Elana said slightly irritated. She was sure she had a ghost but didn't think it killed anyone.

"Let's eat and get out to the place. If there are any ghosts, we'll scare them away," Megan joked. "Are you afraid of ghosts?"

"Not at all, I don't really believe in ghosts and neither does Scott."

They ate their lunch and bought a six pack of sodas and some snacks to take with them and headed for the plantation.

When they turned into the tree lined driveway, Megan gave a low whistle, "Wow, this is awesome. I can't believe you will soon be the owner of this place."

"I know, right. I never in my wildest dreams could have thought I'd one day own such a superb piece of property. Just wait until you see the mansion."

When they got to the clearing at the end of the drive, the mansion loomed ahead like a something out of a picture book.

"Oh my god, Elana, it's beautiful. If it looks as good on the inside as it does from here, I'm going to just cry."

"It does but don't you dare cry."

They parked the car in front and Elana once again saw the old woman but if Megan saw her, she didn't let on.

Chapter 11

Elana and Megan took their time looking at every nook and cranny in the mansion. They talked about how it should be decorated and even decided where the Christmas tree should be placed and how each room should be decorated. They were especially excited to decorate the ballroom.

"I really want to spend a lot of time here," Megan said excitedly as they walked through the house. "I could live in the rooms over the kitchen and you'd never know I was there. I'd be quiet as a mouse."

"You know, I've advertised at the college for a couple of housekeepers to help out for room and board. I thought those rooms would be perfect since they are private."

"You shouldn't have any trouble finding someone. If you don't find anyone, I'm available."

"Do you seriously want to move in? I can cancel the ad," Elana said. "I can't pay anything just yet but room and board should account for something."

"I'd love to. Would it be okay for Darren to live here with me if he helps out too?" Megan asked.

"Of course, we can use all the help we can get."

"Deal then. Our lease is up the end of the month so we won't re-sign it. This will save us a bundle and you'll have live in help. Darren can help Scott with the maintenance and grounds work and I'll take care of inside chores."

"Before you commit, do you mind cooking, laundry, and cleaning in addition to helping with other things?" Elana asked. "That's what I'm advertising for in a housekeeper."

"No problem. I love to cook and I'm pretty good at cleaning and laundry."

"This is perfect. My best friend, a beautiful house, and our careers just getting started together. Couldn't ask for anything better especially since Scott will be getting some help and have a friend here to boot."

"Let's go take a look at the rest of the place. I'm anxious to see the school," Megan said.

"You know, if you and Darren really like it here, maybe you could move into the little house once it's remodeled. What do you think?" Elana suggested. "We could even add on to it if it's not big enough."

"That would be awesome!"

"Let me grab the keys and we'll look at the carriage house first, then the little house and finish with the school building."

They walked down the drive to the carriage house just as a sharp breeze started to blow. Off to the side was a mini whirl wind that dusted them with small pebbles.

"Ouch, that hurts," Megan complained.

"Got us a little devil wind blowing. Wonder where that came from. I don't think it's supposed to rain," Elana said as she unlocked the door to the carriage house. As soon as they went inside the door, the wind seemed to stop.

"This is perfect place for the guys to have a man cave and they can store their boy's toys in the garage," Megan said as she looked at the finished room.

"This room was fixed up as a studio for the previous owner's mother-in-law to paint in. She was on the way to becoming a famous artist when she took sick."

They peeked into the other rooms and the garage portion and then left the carriage house.

"You know, that place kind of gives me the creeps but I never did like garages," Megan said.

"Kind of felt strange to me too. Guess it's because that's where the mother-in-law got sick."

"Over there is the smaller house. It was built at the same time as the mansion for the couple that took care of the school. They were married just after the Civil War. He was a white man and she was a black girl, well not all black, her Daddy was white. I wonder how much trouble that caused them." Elana said.

"I imagine they were shunned by a lot of people around here."

Elana unlocked the front door of the small house and they walked inside.

"This place is in dire need of repair and some real elbow grease. It looks as though no one has lived here for at least 100 years. Look at the woodwork, do you think it could be restored? Those windows look like they have the original glass!" Megan squealed as she looked around.

"I believe that is the original glass, that's impressive. We'll have to be sure to tell the contractors to be very careful with the glass. I want it reused in the replacement windows. I wonder if the mansion still has the original glass."

Megan looked around the downstairs and then carefully navigated the stairs to the second floor. She walked around the rooms and smiled.

"I would love to live in this quaint little house for the rest of my life," she exclaimed. "But I would like a couple of bathrooms, running water, and electricity."

"You can help us with the remodel designs. We're going to need all the creative help we can get. Let's go over to the school. I want you to see the staircase."

As they walked towards the front porch, Elana noticed the boot scrapers on either side of the steps.

"I'm pulling these things out of the ground right now!" she exclaimed as she stooped down to pull each one. "I'll leave them in the school building in case Scott wants them but I sure don't want them where someone might fall and get hurt."

They walked up the steps to the large front porch that extended across the entire front of the building. The first thing they saw as they walked through the door was the massive staircase.

"Oh my god, that's the most beautiful thing I've ever seen!" Megan exclaimed. It looks like those you see in the movies."

"Just think how beautiful it will be once we get it cleaned and painted."

They walked around the downstairs and looked at everything. Megan was more determined than ever to help Elana with this place.

"Did I tell you this was a whore house during the Civil War?" Elana teased.

"No way, I wonder how many men were taken up those stairs," Megan laughed.

"Yep, it was. There was a saloon, tables and a parlor in this area," Elana said as they wandered around the front of the house. "The rooms at the other side were the kitchen and dining area. In back were rooms that were used as bedrooms and at one time a hospital for soldiers. The Confederates were kept on one side of the house and Union soldiers on the other."

They peeked into the kitchen and dining rooms and were amazed that they still looked much the way they probably looked many years ago. Nothing was modernized.

"Let's go upstairs." Elana said as she started up the stairs. "Be careful, I'm not sure how sturdy these old steps are."

"You've got to be kidding, look at these rooms and look at that old rocking chair," Megan shrieked as she looked into one of the bedrooms. "I wonder if there are old maps of the property someplace. There has to be a lot of history here." The chair stopped rocking just before they reached the room.

"I'll ask Mr. Jenkins. I might check at the court house too. There might be some old maps there."

"I'll help you. I love looking up old stuff," Megan volunteered.

"Oh my, look at the time, it's almost 6:00. We better head back home. It'll be dark soon and I have a ton of stuff to get done," Elana said.

"I hate to leave, it seems so peaceful here," Megan said.

"We're going to start moving in next week. The owners said it was all right to move in even though we haven't closed."

"Let me know when and I'll give you a hand. Is anyone else helping you?" Megan asked. "I'm sure Darren will be available, too."

"Scott will be out of town but he said Bill and Al will help so if you and Darren are available too, it shouldn't take too long. I'm anxious to start sleeping in my own home."

"That sounds wonderful, maybe I can stay a couple of nights with you once you get moved in."

"I'd love for you to. We'll be sure to fix up a bedroom just for you. Let's get started home." Elana made sure all the doors were securely locked on the mansion and then she and Megan drove out the driveway.

Elana dropped Megan off at her apartment and stopped by the grocery store to pick up some things she would need for the next few days. She wanted to spend as much time as possible pouring over the journal.

When she got home she curled up on the couch with a sandwich and the journal. She read until around two am and was fascinated by what she was reading.

War started an Miz Bells place always full of soldiers. Most time de be friendly but loud. Miz Bell dint low no fightin at da place so if they get ta fightin they no lowed back so they try ta never fit a bit.

Tonight a bunch of men came and were drunk. They saw ole Jake, Sarah's man and for no reason took him out back and hung him from a tree. Miz Bell made me and Mazy and Luke hide in the barn or they might of hung us too. After ole Jake was dead the men rode off laffin.

Miz Bells niece, Essie, come to live wit her after her family be killed. She sort of strange she dint want anyone to know she be a girl so we had to tend she was a boy. A boy named Willie come wit her and they both joined up with the soldiers. Why she wanted to be

125

a soldier I won't never know. She said somethin bout findin the men who killt her family.

Aint had much time ta do much writin with all helpin take care of sick soldiers and men that stop. Sam been watchin me an I be watchin him. Miz Bell be sweet on one of the rebel officers. Sarah goes bout her work but not smilin no more.

Tonight 3 mean lookin men stopped by and we were all afeard they would want to take us upstairs. We was relieved when Miz Bell tol Sam to give em her specal bottle from uner the bar. When the opium took hold, they were passed out cold and we all be glad. Then Miz Bell tol Sam an Luke to drag em out back.

We heared later that Essie went out to the hog pen an fed em to the hogs before they be clear dead. We all be scared of Essie after that but Miz Bell said those were the men that killt her family an ole Jake. Sarah say they be evil men with evil spirits.

Real sad here. Essie got herself killt and Miz Bell and Mazy be cryin and Sarah be tryin ta comfort dem. Wish this here war be over. Miz Bell and Captin Ashley goin to get hitched up when the war be over and he goin to build her a fine house less he get himself killt.

Elana wondered where the hog pen had been as she read about what that had happened there. She seemed to remember someone telling her there used to be a hog pen where the carriage house stood. She would make a note to ask or research that. *"I wonder if it really was around the carriage house and that's why it feels so strange there."*

Chapter 12

Elana spent the next few days reading Lucy's journal. It was interesting to read about real people who lived on her property so long ago. She could almost feel their excitement, sadness, love, pain and other feelings as she read the words. She wished she could go back to that time for just a day to experience first-hand what she was reading. It was almost time for Scott to get home but she decided she had time to read a few more pages before straightening up the apartment and starting dinner.

War over and Captin Ashbey and Miz Bell tol us they be gettin maried in few weeks. I be settin on da porch dis afternoon lisnin to da birds and Sam come out and set down side me. He said hed had his eye on me for some time and wanted to mary up wit me. I bout fell out the chair. I hed my eye on him too but never thought hed want to mary up wit the likes of me bein a whore an colored an all. He said it dint matter bout da whoren and I be half white. I say yes I would mary up. Mazy be real mad but Luke tol her ta mind her own budness.

Miz Bell and Captin Ashbey got maried in the garden today. There be white folk from all over here. Sam and me snuck over to Preacher Dawsons and got hitched an den came back to da party. No one knew we be maried up cause we dint want to cause a fus for Miz Bell. coloreds and whites aint lowed ta be together.

"Sweetie, I'm home," Scott called as he came through the front door.

"In the kitchen," Elana called back.

Scott dropped his bags and headed to the kitchen. He gathered Elana in his arms a held her tight. "For some reason, I was real worried about you," he said as he held her.

"No need to worry about me, I'm a big girl," Elana laughed a bit embarrassed.

"I got you a belated birthday present. While I was in Boston it occurred to me that we completely passed over your birthday when we got caught up in buying the house. On Sunday I drove to Salem and found the most charming little shop. The woman inside was an elderly black lady dressed in a sweet old fashioned dress. She had pure white hair pulled back into a sort of bun and had a sunbonnet laying on the counter. I told her I needed a special gift for you for your birthday so she reached under the counter and pulled out a long narrow box.

130

"She told me it would be a perfect gift for my beautiful wife. Inside were these two necklaces and she cautioned that we both need to wear these to protect us from evil spirits."

"They're beautiful," Elana exclaimed as she looked at the two necklaces. Each had a gold chain and a small red stone with gold flecks.

"She said the chain was strong and would never break. I wonder what it's made of." Scott said as he took the necklaces out of the box and placed one around Elana's neck and the other around his.

Just then there was a bright red light followed by a blue light that surrounded both Scott and Elana and then disappeared.

"What was that?" Elana said as she laughed nervously.

"I have no idea, maybe it was our field of protection being activated," Scott joked not realizing that was exactly what it was.

Elana felt the chain and noticed the clasp was gone. She looked at the necklace on Scott's neck and saw the clasp on his was also gone. If the chain wouldn't break, they would be wearing these for a long time. *I sure hope they work*, she thought to herself.

"Oh dear, dinner's ruined," Elana cried as she looked at the smoke pouring from the oven.

"Guess we'll have to go out and get something," Scott laughed. "I wanted to take you out for your belated birthday anyway. Where would you like to go?"

"I'll put on some other clothes and we'll go over to the Blue Goose," Elana suggested. "It seems so nice and cozy for an evening meal."

"Sounds good to me."

After they got back from dinner, Scott got into the shower to get ready for bed. Elana padded in and surprised him by getting in the shower with him.

"I've missed you," she said as she lathered his back.

"I missed you too," Scott said as he turned and wrapped his arms around her. "I hope I don't have to travel too much. I hate being away from you so much."

They embraced for a long while and then turned off the shower, dried each other and made their way to the bed to make up for lost time.

The next morning, Scott made pancakes, eggs and bacon for breakfast while Elana made coffee and set the table.

"How was the tour of the property?" Scott asked.

"Wonderful, I invited Megan and Darren to live over the kitchen and help out for their room and board. Hope that's okay with you."

"Sure is, I like both Darren and Megan. It'll be great having them around."

"Megan is interning at the same office as I am so we can ride together and Darren is busy with his parents business so it seemed like a perfect idea. Both can help us around the house and property and it'll be great to have someone around."

Darren is the Director of Operations at his family's business and will one day inherit the business. Even though he spends a lot of time at the office, his main love is riding his four wheeler, hunting and fishing. Scott is an avid hunter and fisherman too so they should get along just fine at the plantation.

"Maybe you should buy a four wheeler. Darren has one and you all could spend a lot of time riding around the fields," Elana offered.

"Good idea. I'll talk to Darren and have him help me pick one out. I want to get out and start exploring as soon as possible"

"I think it might be good to remodel the small house for them to live in once we get settled, what do you think?"

"Good idea. They could be a big help to us and company for you while I'm on the road. I might not worry so much if I knew someone was way out there with you."

"Then it's settled, we'll move in, remodel the small house and have terrific neighbors," Elana squealed.

"I'll be leaving again Saturday for a trip to another of our offices. I'll help you pack as much as I can before I leave. Oh, have you talked with a broker about investments yet?"

"No, I forgot all about that. Why don't we do that this afternoon? I can pack what little stuff we have."

"Okay, I'll call Stan to see if he knows someone reputable."

Scott made an appointment with the investment broker Stan recommended so he and Elana could move most of her money into investment accounts.

They needed to leave enough in the account to cover the cost of the property and incidental expenses but the rest should be earning interest but be accessible.

There were a lot of options open for that amount of money so they decided to trust the advice of the broker for the time being. Once they were settled in, they could research investment options and decide if they needed to make changes.

When they got home that afternoon, Elana showed the pictures she found to Scott.

"You know, if I didn't know better, I'd say this is the same woman that sold me the necklaces," Scott said as he looked at the picture of the elderly black woman. "She's the spitting image of this woman."

"No shit," Elana said nervously. "I have a confession to make. I've been seeing a woman who looks exactly like that woman too."

"So are you telling me we have a ghost?"

"Guess maybe we do," Elana confessed.

"Maybe she's a guardian angel sent to protect us," Scott said as he touched the necklace.

"I think maybe she is. I'm not a bit frightened or uneasy when she's around."

"This plantation is turning into quite an adventure, don't you think?" Scott said as he hugged Elana.

"That it is. It seems like we were destined to find this place and make it our own."

The next morning, Scott packed a few things in his suitcase and headed for the airport once again. Elana started packing their belongings in boxes and dialed Al's number.

"Hi, Al, do you think you could rent a truck for us for tomorrow?" Elana asked when he answered his phone.

"Sure, got any idea how big a truck I'll need to reserve?"

"No idea, use your own judgment. Stop by and I'll give you a credit card to put it on."

"Whoo hoo, I might not come back," Al teased. "I'll stop on my way to the rental company."

"You'll come back, I know where you live," Elana joked. She would trust Al with all her credit cards. She and Scott had known him since they were in first grade and he was one of the best friends a person could have.

"Is Bill going to be able to help out?" Al inquired.

"Yes, but he might be a little late getting here in the morning. He has to take his daughter to the dentist first thing."

"Okay if I bring along one of my buddies then?"

"Sure, we can use all the help we can get."

"See you in a little while to get the card and we should be there tomorrow morning around eight or so."

"K, bye."

Elana hung up and dialed her friend Katie.

"Katie, this is Elana, how are you doing?"

"Great, what's up? I was just thinking about you."

"I have some exciting news, we bought an old plantation near Cantor and would love for you and Kurt to come visit. We're moving in this weekend."

"I'd love to come but not sure if Kurt can get away. How soon will you be ready for company? I have a conference near there coming up soon."

"The sooner the better, I want you to see the place and I think I might have a ghost," Elana confessed.

"Awesome, now my interest is really piqued. I think I might be able to drive down in a week or so for a couple of days."

"I'll email you directions. I can't wait to see you and for you to see this place. I just love it. It has a huge mansion and an old building that used to be a whore house during the Civil War."

"I'll be visiting for sure!" Katie said excitedly. *I wonder if this is the same place Essie talked about. Seems she said her aunt was a madam and the brothel was outside Cantor. Guess I'll see when I get there.*

Chapter 13

The next morning Al, his friend Ken, Darren, and Megan were all at Elana's at 8:00 ready to get started with the move.

Elana had worked most of the night getting as much packed in boxes as she could. She and Megan could finish packing what was left while the guys loaded the furniture and boxes she had ready.

"I didn't realize we had this much stuff," Elana told Megan as they packed. I knew the apartment was full but it's still so small for this much stuff."

"Hope you have lots of beer and pizza laid by for when we're done with this job," Al said as he pulled a dolly into the living room. This looks like a multiple beer and pizza job."

"There'll be enough for a small army and then some," Elana called from the bedroom. "But everything has to be at the new place before we break into the beer."

It didn't take Elana and Megan long to finish packing the rest of the things in boxes so they were able to help load the truck even though they weren't much help. Most of the furniture was too heavy or bulky for them to move.

They wanted to make one trip but it looked like it was going to take at least two to get all of their possessions moved. They took the first load out to the house and unloaded it before lunch and the second one after lunch. Bill arrived just as they were getting ready to leave with the first load.

"I timed that just right," he joked. "Looks like most of the work is done."

"Not even close," Al said. "Have to unload this truckful and come back for a second."

"I'll leave my car here and ride out with one of you if that's all right," Bill said.

"Ride with me," Elana told him. "Al and Ken can ride in the truck and Darren and Megan will take their car."

Elana planned to take them all to the Chips and Chowder for lunch and have pizza delivered for supper. After supper, they could relax at the new house and the guys could drink as much beer as they wanted.

They drove up to the house and Elana unlocked the door so they could get started unloading.

Bill let out a low whistle when he saw the place. "This is an incredible hunk of real estate."

The rest of the guys chimed in and said they would be visiting often especially if Scott let them ride their four wheelers on the property.

"There aren't too many places that we can ride anymore," Al said. "Maybe we can even store our four wheelers here."

"I'm sure you'll be able to ride and leave them here. There's at least 100 acres and I think Darren has already talked Scott into buying a four wheeler so they can ride," Elana said.

Elana told everyone to meet at the Chips and Chowder and she'd spring for lunch. Before they left for the restaurant, she said they could wash up in one of the bathrooms. She was glad the water and electricity hadn't been turned off because she forgot to get it put into her name. First thing Monday morning, she would have to have the utilities put into her name and get the cable and Internet turned on. She couldn't be without her TV and Internet too long. It was going to be boring enough way out here in the country so TV and Internet were a necessity.

When the truck was unloaded, they broke for lunch and all drove back to the restaurant. They had a leisurely lunch and around 2:00 left to pick up the rest of the furniture and boxes.

"Does the refrigerator and stove go?" Bill asked Elana.

"No, those belong to the apartment and the house is already equipped. I hope they're working," she said.

When they came back with the second load, Elana had the guys put the furniture and boxes in the rooms where they belonged so she wouldn't have to try to carry them herself. She and Megan made up the beds and arranged furniture as best as they could. She was glad the windows had blinds because she hadn't gotten around to buying curtains or draperies.

At 5:30, they took the last of the boxes into the house. Elana called in the pizza order and asked to have it delivered. She sent Darren and Bill to the convenience store for a supply of cold beer and sat down on the couch in her new home.

"Darren, are you and Megan staying the night?" Elana asked.

"Yes, but I want to drive back home and get my truck and four wheeler so I can do some exploring tomorrow. Can I ride back with one of you guys?"

"Sure," Bill said, "I go right by your place." Bill had driven his car back when they brought the last load out to the property.

"Scott is going to be so disappointed to miss all this," Elana said.

Elana found paper plates, silverware and napkins and put them on the table next to the pizza. She had Darren put the beer in the refrigerator and told everyone to help themselves.

After everyone had eaten, they talked for a while and then all but Megan and Elana left. Darren said he would be back before it got dark.

"Darren, bring my toothbrush, toothpaste clean underwear, shorts, tee shirt and a house coat and whatever you'll need for the night when you come back. Oh, bring some sheets, pillows, blankets and towels."

"Okay, if you think of anything else, call."

"Just look around and bring anything else you think we might need."

"I'll be back later, anything you want from the store?"

"No, I think we have everything for right now."

"Let's just relax the rest of the evening," Elana told Megan. "I think we have enough stuff unpacked and set up for the night. I'm beat. It's going to be wonderful to just sit and relax."

"Sure is," said Megan as she collapsed in one of the chairs. "Sure wish we had cable."

"We have some movies if you want to pick one out," Elana said pointing to one of the boxes.

"Good idea but I'll wait until Darren gets here so we can all watch together."

"I'm going to check the doors and windows and make sure they are all locked. Want to go with me."

"Yeah, wait up," Megan said as she dragged herself out of the chair.

They walked around the entire house checking locks on all the windows and doors and all were secure. "I didn't know there were so many windows and doors in this place," Elana said as she checked the last door."

"Just wait until you decide to wash all those windows," Megan laughed.

"Don't remind me. Did I tell you about the journal written by a woman who lived here years ago?" Elana asked Megan.

"No, have you read it yet?"

"I've started but it's faded and difficult to read. But, the small house was built for the woman and her husband."

"No way, can I see the book?"

"Sure, it's here somewhere," Elana said digging in one of the boxes.

"Here it is. There's a picture of her and her husband too."

"Where did you find it?"

"It found me. Scott's boss is the woman's great, great, great grandson. Small world huh."

"She worked in the whore house until the Civil War was over and they closed it. The madam got married and they opened a school for young women in place of the brothel. Her husband built this house for them and the small house for Lucy and her husband. Lucy was a mulatto and her husband was a white man and was the bartender in the brothel."

"Quite a colorful bunch of people. Wouldn't it be awesome to go back to that time for a while."

"I would love to, but just for a while. Don't think I could get along too long without all the modern conveniences."

"I think I'm going to have a dinner party in a couple of weeks and invite Scott's boss and his wife along with you all, Bill, Al and their girlfriends."

"I doubt that Bill and Al will come but it sure sounds like fun. Are you going to cook for that many people?"

"No way, the Chips and Chowder caters so I'll hire them. I can hardly cook for Scott and me let alone a bunch of people."

"Okay if I read this when you don't have your nose in it?"

"Of course, I'm sure you'll want to know all about the people that lived in your house."

"Sounds like Darren's back," Megan said when she saw lights coming up the drive. "He's real excited to have a place to ride and someone to ride with."

Darren got out of the truck and unloaded his four wheeler. All right if I put this in the carriage house?"

"Yeah, I'll get the keys and we'll meet you there," Elana said.

Megan and she walked down to the carriage house while Darren drove the four wheeler down. She unlocked the door to the garage and switched on the light. As she walked into the garage, she felt the necklace on her neck tingle. *Wonder why it did that*, she thought to herself.

Darren drove the four wheeler into the garage and then turned out the lights, locked the door and they walked back to the house together.

"I'm going to do some serious exploring after breakfast tomorrow. Anyone want to ride along? Should be a lot of fun."

"I'm going to finish unpacking," Elana said.

"I'm going to help her," Megan said. She didn't like riding behind Darren because he seemed to take too many risks.

"Suit yourselves, but you're going to miss some serious fun."

They got back to the house, opened some beers and Elana put in a movie that Megan had found. When the movie was over, they decided to turn in so they could get an early start the next morning.

Just as Elana was climbing into bed, Scott called. She was hoping he'd call this evening. She didn't call him because she wasn't sure what his schedule would be and didn't want to interrupt any meetings.

"Hi Sweetie," Scott said when she answered the phone.

"Hi, I sure do miss you."

"I've only been gone a day but I miss you too. Did you get everything moved in?"

"Yes and we're staying the night here. The apartment is empty so I won't be staying there anymore."

"By we, do you mean Darren and Megan?"

"Yes, we set up one of the bedrooms for them and they are going to stay until you get home. Darren has already brought his four wheeler over. He's going to explore some of the property tomorrow. Both him and Megan are excited about this place and all the possibilities. I think I'm as excited as they are."

"Oh man, I wish I was there so I could go with him. I'm going to buy one as soon as I can. I can't wait to look the place over. How did we ever luck into such a wonderful place?"

"When do you think you will get some time off to relax?" Elana asked.

"Who knows, I guess as soon as they feel I know the ropes of the new position."

"Oh, I'm planning to have a dinner party in a couple of weeks and want to invite Stan and his wife. I think they'll enjoy seeing the place and hearing what I've read in his grandmother's journal."

"Great, I'll tell him. He's pretty excited about you reading the journal and about us buying the plantation. I gotta go now, Stan is coming by to go over some paperwork in a few minutes," Scott said.

"Do you ever get to sleep?" Elana laughed.

"Not much and I'm so beat. I can't wait to get home and get a good night's sleep with you beside me. Love you, bye."

"Love you too. Call me tomorrow."

"Okay, bye."

Elana turned off the light and tried to go to sleep but was restless for some reason.

The next morning, everyone was up at the crack of dawn. Elana made eggs, bacon, toast and coffee for breakfast and made a mental note to go grocery shopping later.

As soon as Darren ate, he took the keys to the carriage house and got out his four wheeler. He parked it in front of the house and then showered and got ready for his ride.

He took a couple of sodas with him and headed out to explore the property. He drove past the carriage house and barn and headed towards what he hoped was the property line to the south. He rode for about a half hour when he saw the remains of a car wrecked into a tree.

"What the…" he said to no one in particular. "How'd that get here?"

He rode closer and saw there were weeds grown all around the car so he knew it had been here for some time.

When he got near the back of the car, he turned off the motor and went to have a look. As he got close to the driver's door, he saw the window was down and the steering wheel and dashboard was almost in the front seat.

"Oh hell no," he screamed. "No!" In the front seat under the dashboard was a skeleton. The airbag was partially covering the skeleton but he could see enough to know what he was seeing. He forced himself to look in the rest of the car but didn't see anything else to indicate there was more than one person.

"This is too fucked up, I'm getting out of here," he said a he ran back to his four wheeler as fast as he could.

He jumped on his four wheeler, started the engine and high-tailed it back to the house. When he got to the front porch, he shouted for Megan and Elana.

"What's wrong," they both said at once as the stepped out on the porch.

"Call 911, there's a body in a car down in that field."

"Oh shit," Elana said. "How do you know they're dead?"

"Because all that's left is a skeleton."

"Oh shit," Elana said again as she dialed 911.

"911, what's your emergency?" the dispatched inquired.

"There's a wrecked car on my property and the person inside is dead."

"How do you know they're dead?" the dispatcher again inquired.

"Because all that's left is a skeleton," Elana repeated what Darren had told her.

"Are there any other victims or injuries?"

"No."

"What's your name, mam?

"Elana Palmer."

"What's the address?"

"10498 St. Rt. 2."

"I'll dispatch the sheriff. Someone should be there shortly. Did you touch anything?"

"Darren, did you touch anything?" Elana asked.

"Hell no, I just got out of there."

"No, we didn't."

"All right, the sheriff has been notified and will be there in a few minutes. Do you want me to stay on the line with you?"

"No, we'll watch for the sheriff."

About 15 minutes later, they heard the siren and then saw the sheriff turning into the driveway. Behind him were an ambulance and a rollback car carrier.

When the sheriff got out of his car, everyone started talking at once.

"Whoa, slow down. I'm Joe. Who found the body?" the sheriff asked.

"I did, Joe," Darren answered. "It's in a wrecked car down in that field. Looks like it's been there a long time but the car is last year's model."

"Doesn't take long for a body to decompose in this weather," the sheriff answered. "Can I get there in my car?"

"I think so, the ground is pretty level and there aren't too many rocks," Darren volunteered. "You can ride with me on my four wheeler if you want."

"No, we'll follow you."

Darren started his four wheeler and led the procession to the spot where the wrecked car sat.

The sheriff got out of his car and walked over to the vehicle. "Wonder what he was doing driving down here?" he muttered.

He walked around to the passenger side of the car and reached in through the open window to the glove box. The vehicle was registered to Michael Ranson. He saw what looked like brochures from Baxter Properties in the back seat along with a cooler.

"Oh shit, I wonder if this is Deb's missing agent," he said to no one in particular as he dialed Debra's phone.

"Deb, Joe here, I think we might have found your missing agent."

"You mean Mike?" she asked.

"Yeah, he's out here at the LaBelle property."

"Well put him on the phone, I have a few things to say to him."

"Afraid I can't do that, he's dead."

"What!" Debra screamed.

The sheriff pulled the phone away from his ear and then said, "Yep, found his wrecked car in a field behind the house. Been here a long time from the looks of him."

"He didn't come back after the open house a year ago. Oh dear, I wonder if he's been there all this time and we didn't know it."

"Looks like it. Still not sure how he got clear down here when the road is the other direction. Guess that'll be a mystery."

Chapter 14
August the Previous Year

Michael Ranson was arrogant, self-centered, unreliable, and one of the best real estate salesmen Debra had ever seen. He consistently was the top salesman every month and his yearly income was in the six figures. For this reason, she gave him the LaBelle listing. If he couldn't sell the place, no one could.

Mike didn't like to do open houses but Cory Jenkins, owner of LaBelle, insisted they hold an open house at least every other month. Mike usually didn't book open houses in August but this year he had missed July so he didn't have much choice. Mike reluctantly loaded his car with his laptop and a cooler full of sodas and beer, sandwiches, and other snacks. He didn't let Debra know about the beer. He always loaded his sandwiches with garlic so no one could smell the alcohol over the smell of the garlic.

He kept a supply of brochures and business cards in his car but didn't take the standard supply of cookies and drinks Debra thought should be available for would-be clients at an open house.

"No need to take any extra food, no one is going to show up anyway," he told Debra the morning before leaving for the open house. He seemed to know which houses would have traffic and which wouldn't and this one definitely wouldn't have any traffic.

"You should take something just in case," she insisted but he just shrugged his shoulders and walked out and got into his car. He drove a brand new sports car, completely paid for and 'fast as the wind' as he liked to say.

"Check in this evening," Debra called not sure if he heard or not.

Mike got to the property around 11:00 that morning and put up the signs and balloons then drove back to the house. He didn't bother unlocking the house since he could always open up if someone showed up. He sat on the porch for a while and then went out back to take a quick leak. That was one perk with being way out here in the country, he could get back to nature without anyone noticing.

It was lunch time so he moved to his car where the seat was much more comfortable. He took one of the sandwiches from the cooler and popped a can of beer to drink while he ate.

"Whew, I should have gone a bit easy on the garlic. Guess I'll have to drink the whole six pack to get the taste of this stuff out of my mouth."

The day was sort of cool even though it was August so he sat in his car and surfed the web on his tablet. He chatted with a few girls, emailed some of his friends and surfed a few porn sites. Before he realized it, it was late afternoon.

Where did the time go? Must be having fun, he thought sarcastically. *Think I'll text Sheila and see if she wants to go out this evening.*

Just then, he saw what he thought was black smoke coming from behind the old carriage house. He watched it curl up and swirl around the building and then he heard laughter.

What the ... he said to himself as he started to get out of the car to go investigate.

He had just gotten out when the black smoke turned into shadows that quickly swirled up and over his car. He jumped back in and shut the door to try to keep it out but soon the shadows were swirling in and out of the car and all around it all the while laughing an evil laugh.

"I gotta get out of here," he screamed as he started the car and peeled out of the parking space.

He drove as fast as he could down the drive. All at once, he saw that he was passing the house going in the opposite direction from the main road. He was then passing the carriage house, the barn, and going down through the field. He looked down and saw the speedometer was measuring over 90 miles an hour. He tried to put on the brake but the car kept going faster.

The trees in the field were a blur as he raced ahead at breakneck speed. "STOP! STOP!" he shouted but the car didn't slow down. He tried turning off the key but the car didn't slow down. The shadows kept swirling faster and faster in and out of the windows and around the car. Their laughter drove Mike crazy. He tried to cover his ears to drown out the sound but it only made it louder. He tried to close his eyes but instinct told him to watch where he was going.

"Oh God, what's happening," he moaned. "Fuck, fuck, fuck!" he screamed.

In front of him, he could see the huge oak tree and knew he was on a collision course if he didn't turn the wheel. Try as he might, the wheel wouldn't turn. He hit the tree going at least a 120 miles an hour. The front of the car wrapped around the tree pushing the motor and interior into the passenger area. Mike was pinned to his seat by the steering wheel and dashboard, the air bag covered his upper body. He didn't die immediately, and was able to pull the air bag from his face. As he sat there in shock, he saw the shadows swirling around the car and heard the evil laughter.

Oh my god, I'm going to die, he thought as tears rolled down his cheeks. He lived for a few hours in shear panic and shock. *I wonder why I don't feel any pain,* he said to himself between sobs. He didn't realize the motor had pushed the interior of the car against his body and had sealed off his lower body. His spine and entire lower body was crushed and he was dying a slow death. He sat there trying to look around but everything kept drifting off.

"I wonder where my cell phone is?" he said in a panic. "If I can find it, I can call someone." He turned his head as much as he could to look around the car but was unable to see anything because the dashboard and air bag was resting on the passenger seat.

He thought he felt the car move and wondered if someone was there to help. The car did move but only to release some of the pressure the motor was putting on his body. When it moved, his insides spilled out as he felt a severe stab of pain and was dead within seconds.

The shadows swirled around and around above the car and then flew back to the carriage house where they disappeared into the ground through a crevice in some rocks, laughing the whole time.

Monday morning, Debra tried calling Mike's cell phone but the call went to voicemail. She hadn't heard anything from him since he left Saturday morning but that wasn't unusual. It was unusual that he didn't answer his phone on a workday.

"Mike, this is Deb, call me when you get this. I'm starting to worry about you," she said to his voice mail. "I wonder where he has gotten off to now," she said to no one in particular. "I was he was more reliable."

When she hadn't heard from him by 2:00, she decided to drive by his apartment to see if his car was there. When she didn't see his car there, she decided to drive out by the LaBelle property to see if he might have left any paperwork from the open house.

When she drove up to the mansion, she didn't see his car so she went into the house. There was nothing in the foyer so she walked back to her car disgusted. *He's probably relaxing on a beach somewhere. He'll come back when he feels like working again*, Debra thought as she drove back to the office.

When Jett stopped by the office late that afternoon, Debra turned the listing for LaBelle property over to her. Jett wasn't nearly as good a salesperson as Mike but she was reliable and put everything she had into trying to sell her listings.

When that no good little bastard comes back, I'm going to fire him on the spot, Debra thought to herself. She knew she wouldn't because Mike brought in a lot of income for her but she was so angry right now.

Chapter 15

Elana could hardly wait for Scott to call that evening. She wanted to fill him in on the wrecked car and ask when he was coming home. She supposed she could call him but was reluctant to do so since it wasn't an emergency. Just then her phone rang. She looked at the caller ID and immediately answered it.

"Oh Scott, I'm so glad you called," she said breathlessly.

"I call every evening," he said somewhat irritated.

"I know but I still wonder if you'll have time. Darren was riding his four wheeler today and found a wrecked car on the property and there was a body inside. Actually it was a skeleton. According to the identification in the car, it was one of Debra's agents that was out here last year for an open house."

"What!" Scott shouted. "Tell me all about and don't leave out any details. Should I come home right now?

"We're fine and everything is under control. The sheriff said he went missing after holding an open house. Debra thought he had just gone on a vacation or something since he wasn't real reliable. She's pretty upset."

"How did he happen to wreck on the property and no one see it?"

"No one knows, his car hit a tree on the other side of the field past the carriage house and barn. The opposite direction from the road. Strange why he would drive down there."

"Real strange. Did the sheriff think there was foul play involved? The last thing we need is a murder out there."

"No, he said it was an accident but not sure how. Guess we'll never know. When are you coming home?"

"Tomorrow and Stan says there won't be much more, if any, traveling this year and I'm really glad. I want to get to work on what they hired me to do, not jet around the country."

"I'll be glad to have you home nights. It gets mighty lonesome here without you."

"I should be at the airport around 1:00 tomorrow afternoon and home by around 3:00. Let's eat out at the Chips and Chowder restaurant. I'm kind of hungry for some seafood."

"Sounds good to me. I don't feel much like cooking until I get the kitchen stocked and equipped the way I want it."

"Oh, Stan said he was anxious to come to a dinner party and look the place over. I don't think he has ever seen the property."

"He's in for a real treat. I don't think the house where his grandmother lived has been occupied since she lived there."

"Gotta go, we have some things to go over before bedtime. See you tomorrow. Love you."

"Love you too, bye."

Darren and Megan were still out so Elana got the journal and started to read. The cable guy was to be there tomorrow morning so she didn't have TV yet and didn't really miss it since she had the journal.

Doctor say baby Isaacs fever broke. I been so scared hed die like da other babys I got buried in the grave yard out back. Babys don't seem to get over da sickness

He been sleepin all day but doctor say that good to heal him. Miz Bell brung us stew for supper an Sam helped Captin Ashbey cut some wood.

Baby Isaac better now. He up runnin an playin. He done brung a big bug in da kitchen an tried to scare me. I tended ta be scared an he gigled. Baby Isaac look jest like he daddy, even he skin be white.

Sam laid up now with amonia. I jest know he gonna die he so sick. He been sleepin for 3 days now an so hot I can harly stand to touch him. Doctor give him some medcin and tol me to give him a dose ever 4 hours.

Sarah took baby Isaac to her cabin til Sam dies or get better.

We buried Sam side our 3 babies. The grave yard gettin full. Sarah say she be buried side old Jake. Mazy tol Miz Bell that her and Luke are movin to Georgie to be close to his family if he can find em. I gonna miss Mazy even though she always mad at me. Isaac gonna miss luke now that he pappy be ded.

I be missin sam. Make me so sad

Miz Bell had a baby boy today. Captin Ashbey was proud as he could be. Said he wish Sam cud see him. Captin Ashbey liked Sam. Baby Lillian sure do like her lil brother.

Elana went to the kitchen to get a soda when she heard a car outside. She hurried back to the front of the house to see who was there hoping it was Darren and Megan.

"Elana, we're home," Megan announced from the foyer. They were all in the habit of announcing when they came into the house.

"In here," Elana called from the old ballroom. They were using the old ballroom as a great room since it was large enough for everyone to be able to do whatever they might want to do.

"I told the property manager we wouldn't be renewing our lease," Darren announced. "So if it's okay, we can move in anytime and start helping out. Our apartment was furnished so we don't have too much to move."

160

"Great," Elana said. "Scott will be home tomorrow and said he won't be traveling any more for the rest of the year so we can fix up the rooms over the kitchen for you or you can stay in the room you have now. Your choice."

"I'd like the rooms over the kitchen," Megan said. "It would seem like our own apartment and we wouldn't bother you and Scott too much. You probably wouldn't even know we were here most of the time."

"That's what I was thinking, at least until we get the old house remodeled and ready for you to move in," Elana said.

"I can work on the house on the weekends and after work if it's okay," Darren offered.

"We'll take a look at it and see what needs done and get started. Maybe you can have it ready by the holidays," Elana told him.

"Wouldn't that be super?" Megan giggled. "Our own home for the holidays. Maybe I could invite our parents and have an old fashioned Christmas."

"Don't get carried away," Darren cautioned. Her parents didn't approve of them living together without out a marriage license and didn't mind telling them at any opportunity.

"Well, maybe your parents then," Megan laughed.

"Nope, I want to spend Christmas alone with you in our new house, if I can get it ready by then."

Megan hugged him and said, "Let's go up to bed, I'm beat."

"Night you two," Elana called as they headed for the stairs.

"Night," both chimed together between giggles.

Elana checked the front door to make sure it was locked. She had already checked all the other windows and doors out of habit. Even though she had only been here a few days, she felt this was a ritual she would continue for a long time.

She decided to take the journal upstairs and read some more before going to sleep so she turned off the lights except for one in the foyer and went upstairs.

I be settin on da porch stringin beans when I see Sarah makin a fire in the fire pit to het water for her worsh. All a sudden, she turned an her dress tail hit a hot coal and her dress got fire. She went screamin an runnin but she be all flames. Captin Ashbey run out and beat the flames wit his hands to put it out. She lived for two days and was in so much pain. Captin Ashbey burned his hands an the doctor said it would be a long time afor dey healed.

Sarah be wit jake now. She be happy agin fer sure

Captin Ashbey hired a hand to work now that Sam be dead an Luke be gone. Jimmy keep lookin at me an I keep lookin at him. Be nice ta have a man round the house agin. Isaac be big nuf ta help out but Captin Ashbey needs a man to do da hard work.

162

Me an Jimmy got maried up taday. Folks round here take better ta me now that I be with my own kind. isaac likes jimmy and they work the fields an go huntin. Jimmy even go to church wit me and issac.

Isaac left for school today. He gonna be a lawyer in the city when he done with hes studies. I gonna miss him but he say he will write to me. Seems like everyone be leavin or dyin.

I be lonesome wit out Isaac round

Miz Bell tol me and Jimmy they be sellin the place. Her and Captin Ashbey caint run the school no more an dey want to move to Caroliny near the ocean. Miz Bell say she doin it for Essie but not sure why. Essie be dead so how can she move for her. She tol me Essie always wanted ta see the ocean so she was goin ta see it for her.

It was after 1:00 when Elana closed the journal and switched off the light to go to sleep. She slept fitfully thinking about Lucy and the hardships she must have endured. She couldn't even imagine how difficult it must have been to have lived back then. It seemed like they worked so hard and some died of even minor illnesses.

When Elana dragged herself out of bed the next morning, Megan and Darren were already up and eating breakfast. Megan had made French toast, eggs and sausage patties. Elana grabbed a plate and filled it full.

She was starving for some reason. Probably because she didn't have to cook the food.

"This is delicious, Megan," Elana said.

"Thought I'd get started on my job here," she grinned.

"Guess you're the chief cook and bottle washer," Elana joked.

"And I'm the handyman," Darren chimed in.

"Yep," Elana agreed.

"Megan, let's go shopping this morning and get whatever you think we need for the kitchen along with some groceries. We can't eat out all the time. Is there a washer and dryer in the laundry closet?"

"I haven't looked," Megan said as she walked over to the closet and opened the door.

To their surprise, there was a beautiful washer and dryer set along with detergent, bleach, stain removers and other laundry supplies. There were also baskets, pins, clothesline, and an ironing board with an iron.

"Darren, will you be around this morning? The cable guy is coming to hook up the cable for us," Elana inquired.

"I can be. I can call off work since I'm pretty much in charge. Where do you want them put?"

"I think at least two connections in each room except for the foyer, dining room and bathrooms. What do you think?" Elana said. "If you think there should be more, tell the guy. Better to have too many than not enough."

164

"I'll have a look around and see where we need them," Darren said. "Do you want any in the carriage house or just this house?"

"Just this house. If you and Scott make a man cave in the carriage house later, we can have the guy come back," Elana laughed.

"I hadn't thought of a man cave but that's a good idea. We could put in a refrigerator, a big screen TV, maybe a pool table…hummm. I'll have to talk to Scott."

"Guys," Megan said as she rolled her eyes. "Elana and I are going to make the old school building into a spa so you can have the old carriage house."

Elana smiled. It was fun having Megan and Darren there. She couldn't wait for Scott to get home so he could be part of it.

Chapter 16

After Elana and Megan returned from their shopping trip and had all the groceries stored away, Elana sat down with the journal to wait for Scott to get home. Darren was still working with the cable guy and Megan was busy looking at the rooms over the kitchen to decide how she wanted them decorated. Life seemed so good to Elana at this moment.

The new owners tol Miz Bell that me an Jimmy kin stay on an take care of da place if we want. They wud pay us some an let us live in da house rent free for cleanin the big house an school an keepin the grounds. We be glad caus we got no place else ta go. I dont want ta leave my babies and Sam even though they be dead. Jimmy say he like it here to

Isaac is finishin up school and got a job with a law office in the city. He comin home in a month or so but caint stay. Has ta live in the city. Tol me he gettin maried too. He marin up wit a white woman. He say ever one think he white an he don tell no diferent

New owners makin lots of changes ta the property. They gonna move the hog pen to behind the barn cause of the smell. Gonna build a carriage house ta keep their buggys. Men supposed ta be here nex week ta start on it. Don't understand them startin in the hot August sun.

Jimmy be watchin the men tear down the hog pen and fence when one of the men seen a big hole open in the ground. He hollered at the man nearest the hole but it be to late. It swollered up the man Jimmy say he could hear laughin then da man screamin and den all at once he quit and da hole filled back up. Left a hole tween 2 rocks dat no one would go near

Jimmy say he thought it be haints made the hole and covered it back up. I dint tell him bout Essie killin the men on that very spot.

Elana decided to walk out to the carriage house to see if she could see where the rock opening was. When she got there, she found it behind the carriage house and looked closely at it.

All at once the necklace started to vibrate. It shook so hard she thought it would fall off her neck. *This is the strangest thing I've ever felt*, she thought as she touched the stone to stop the vibrations. *I wonder what's in that hole. Whatever it is, I hope this thing protects me from it.* The necklace vibrated the entire time she was standing near the crevice.

She walked around to the other side of the carriage house and then down to the barn. She looked back to the house and was amazed at how beautiful it looked. She felt there was something wrong with the place and was determined to find out what it was and correct it. She just didn't know where to start or what to do.

I wonder if there are any more dead bodies around here, she thought to herself. *I wonder where that cemetery is. I'm going to have to search around for the cemeteries.* She walked into the barn and looked around and was surprised that the necklace didn't vibrate.

She left the barn and looked back to the house. She saw Darren and the cable guy coming out the front door and decided to hold off on her explorations for the time being. Darren saw her and motioned her to come to where they were talking. She could see they were both smiling and talking a mile a minute.

"He's all through and looks like we have excellent signal in every room. We have Internet too. It comes with the package so we're all set," Darren said.

"Now we have to buy some more TVs," Elana said.

"You all have one and Megan and me have one so that's all we need for now or at least until we build the man cave," Darren teased.

"If you have any problems, call the office and I'll come back and fix them," the cable guy told Darren. "I put all new wiring and hardware in so you shouldn't have any but you never know on a job this big. If I'd known there was this much work, I'd have brought a helper. Thanks for giving me a hand Darren. If you ever need a job, I'll put in a good word for you at the office."

"I might just take you up on that someday," Darren offered. "I didn't realize how much fun this type of work was."

"Have a good day, Ma'am," the cable guy said as he rolled his eyes and tipped his hat to Elana.

He drove down the drive just as Scott was driving in.

Elana and Darren stood on the porch waiting for Scott to park.

"I see we have cable," Scott said as he got out of his car.

"Yes and Internet," Elana said as she ran over and hugged him. "So glad your home, I've missed you so much."

"Good to be home even if I haven't hardly been here."

"Hey old buddy, welcome back," Darren said as he extended his hand to shake Scott's. "You sure did miss some excitement. Not sure I'm ever going to go exploring alone again. Finding a body sort of puts the fear of God in a person," Darren laughed nervously.

"We'll have to explore the whole place to see if there are any more bodies lurking around," Scott joked."

"Nope, one's enough for this old boy's lifetime. Not sure what I'd do if we ran across another one. Probably go a bit insane or just get drunk and never sober up."

"I do want to go look about a four wheeler this weekend if you can go with me. I don't know a thing about buying one but it sure will be fun to ride over the property."

"I'm free, not sure what the girls have planned."

"Elana and I are going to the Chips and Chowder for dinner, you and Megan want to tag along?"

"I would love to but have to ask Megan. She might have plans that she hasn't told me about," Darren said.

Just then Megan came out the front door. "Welcome home stranger," she said to Scott.

"Good to be home."

"Honey, do you want to go to the Chips and Chowder with Elana and Scott tonight?"

"That would be fantastic. I don't feel like cooking and the food there is delicious."

"Let's get ready and go, I'm starved," Scott said.

They got back home from dinner around 8:30 and settled in to watch TV. Megan and Elana made popcorn and brought in some beers for everyone. They all settled on the huge couch and got ready for a relaxing evening.

"Let's watch something funny," Darren suggested. "I've seen enough sad stuff to last a lifetime."

Scott flipped through the channels and they settled on a popular sitcom. After a couple of hours of TV, Darren and Megan decided to call it a night and went up to their room. Scott and Elana sat for a while catching up, glad to finally be alone. Sometimes it was difficult to be alone anymore.

171

"I'm just about finished reading the journal," Elana told Scott. "I'm amazed at how life was back then and its more amazing to know that it was lived right here."

"Wish I had the patience to read it. I know I'd get frustrated if I couldn't make out every word."

"Let's go up to bed. You haven't even seen our new bedroom and it needs to be broken in in the worst way," Elana said as she got up from the couch.

Scott turned off the TV, switched off the lights and started to follow her up the stairs.

"Check to be sure the doors locked," Elana reminded him.

"Yep, locked up tight. Did anyone check the kitchen door?"

"Yes, I made sure it was locked while we were making the popcorn."

Together they walked up the stairs hand in hand.

"Well if this room don't beat all," Scott said as he looked around the huge bedroom.

"Check out the bathroom," Elana said with a giggle.

She had placed candles all around and there was a bottle of wine in an ice bucket along with 2 glasses. When they got to the bathroom, she started water in the tub and lit the candles.

"Are you trying to seduce me?" Scott teased.

"Nope, I'm gonna seduce you, not try to so don't even try to run!"

172

They undressed each other and stepped into the tub. Scott opened the wine and poured each a glass and they lay back in each other's arms enjoying a relaxing calm.

When they got out of the tub, Scott carried her to the bed where they made passionate love before falling asleep cuddled together.

The next morning Scott slipped out of bed without waking Elana. He showered and started out the door when she woke up.

"Trying to slip away, mister?"

"No, just thought you might want to sleep in."

"I'll be down as soon as I shower. Tell Megan to save some breakfast for me."

Megan had a full breakfast on the table along with juice and hot coffee.

"This looks delicious, Megan," Scott bragged. "Where's Darren?"

"He'll be down in a bit. Scott, I'm kind of worried. Do you think there are any more bodies around here?" Megan questioned.

"I doubt it. The real estate agents were accidents that could have happened anywhere. I don't think we have anything to worry about," Scott said trying to comfort her. "It's always uncomfortable at a new place. Once you get used to the place, you'll feel better."

"I hope so. I love it here and I'm so anxious to get the little house fixed up for me and Darren."

173

"Yeah, I want to go over that with you and Darren. I think we should get started as soon as possible since it won't be that long before bad weather sets in."

Elana and Darren walked into the kitchen and sat down at the table.

"Morning everyone," Darren said as he filled his plate. "Woman, you're going to make me fat cooking like this."

"Oh, we'll think of ways to burn the fat off," Megan teased as she poured the coffee for everyone.

"Darren and I are going four wheeler shopping after breakfast," Scott announced.

"I'm going to visit my sister," Megan said. "Want to tag along Elana?"

"No, I'm going to relax with the journal. I'm almost finished reading it and I think we're about to get pretty busy around here."

"OK, guess we'll all meet back here this afternoon," Scott said.

Chapter 17

After everyone had left Elana got a glass of iced tea and settled in to get lost in Lucy's journal. She wanted to spend more time with Scott but welcomed the time alone this morning to read.

da workers started tearin down da cabin where Mazy an Luke lived. It sad to see it go. I got nothin to remind me of Mazy. wish she would write more often. Last letter I got be 3 month ago. They tear down Sarahs cabin next. Place won't be da same but Jimmy and me caint afford ta leave. Don't know where wed go.

be feelin mighty blue today so think I go in d lil room an sit wit my babys an Sams things. Hope Jimmy dont come back while I be there. He dont know bout the room and he wuldnt unerstan bout Sams things. Captin Ashbey built hiddn rooms in both houses so if outlaws come, we can hide. There be 2 rooms in da school to but I dont think da owner knows bout any of em. Miz Bell say not ta tell em. She don like to give away her secret places to strangers

Sure is hot even for August. Workers still buildin the carriage house. masta Thomas goes out every day to make sure they be workin. He a mean one. He never say much to Jimmy or me but we be careful ta do as we told an not sass. I think he thinks we his slaves but he don beat us

Strange thing happen today. I be watchin the workers out the window when black smoke come flyin out from hind the carriage house. One of da workers started wavin his arms and da smoke turned into 3 shados. The shados flew round an round the worker laughin the hole time

The worker fell to da ground and the shados swirled even faster. The man screamed and screamed while the others just stood an watched too afeared ta do anything. All at once the man run up da ladder to da roof an fell off. soon as he hit da ground, the shados swirled round him for da longest time, laughin an evil laugh and den flew to behind da carriage house and disapeared.

Masta Thomas be real mad one of da men died. I tol Jimmy what hapened an he look real scared. He say it be haints and we need be real careful to stay away from da carriage house. da other workers left after the undertaker took da body away and didn't come back today. Masta Thomas was real mad bout that too.

Masta Thomas says they is closin da school. He say Jimmy and me have ta find someplace else ta live. I dont want to leave my babies and Sam. Isaac say we can live wit him an his family but I don want to do dat. He be passin as white an we jest get him trubl. He say Jimmy can get a job in the city an I can take care of his babies an the house but I say no. We gon ta look round som of da hors farms ta see if jimmy can get on. I dont want to leave my babies and Sam but I have ta. I be so sad.

"That seems to be all she's written. I wonder what the rest of her life was like," Elana said out loud to no one in particular. "I hope Stan knows more about her."

I wonder what's at the carriage house, Elana thought. *I wonder if that's why this necklace vibrates when I go out there. I need to talk to Scott about this. Strange that this started in August and both real estate agents died in August. I wonder when Mr. Jenkins' mother-in-law went crazy in the carriage house.* Elana had lots of unanswered questions.

She closed the journal and placed it on the stand beside the couch and went to the kitchen for another glass of iced tea. She walked around the kitchen pushing on the walls trying to decide if there was a hidden room there but decided there wasn't. *I wonder where they hid them.*

"Elana, I'm back," Megan called from the foyer.

177

"In the kitchen, Megan."

"Whew, I didn't know visiting my sister was going to be so traumatic. She and Blake are separating and she is frantic. I told her to just go out and get drunk but she started quoting scriptures. No wonder Blake left."

"They seemed mismatched to me when I met them last Christmas. Guess opposites don't always attract and if they do, they don't last."

"Tell me about it. I should have known better than to go visit. Seems like it's always a downer."

"Well, I have an upper for you. I read in the journal that there are hidden rooms in both houses and the school. We can go searching while Darren and Scott are exploring." Elana didn't tell her about the shadows. She wanted to talk to Scott about that first.

"So, did she say where these rooms were?"

"Not even a little clue but she said she stored stuff from her dead babies and her husband in the one in the little house. Maybe the stuff is still there."

"So she had dead babies, how many?"

"Two or three. Her husband and the babies are buried somewhere on the property in a family cemetery. There's also a couple of old slaves buried there too. Don't know if anyone else is there though."

"Interesting. We have some exploring of our own to do. I love the history of this place. I should have majored in history instead of psychology," Megan said wistfully. "Maybe I'll take some courses in history sometime."

"We need to go furniture shopping before our internship starts and we only have a little over a week left," Elana announced as she looked at the tattered old couch and chair in the TV room. "I want to have the place looking spiffy for our dinner party."

"You need some dining room furniture too. I don't think the old dinette set classifies as spiffy," Megan laughed.

"Scott and Darren will be working next week so let's shop till we drop."

"We can start with that new furniture store down by the bank. We should be able to find some really nice stuff there. I'd like to buy some furniture for the rooms over the kitchen that I can move to the other house when it's remodeled. I think you and Scott could use some privacy and I'm tired of trying to be quiet so the sooner we move into those rooms the better," Megan laughed.

"Yeah, your moaning drives me crazy after I finally figured out what it was," Elana teased. "I never knew anyone as vocal as you."

"Here come Darren and Scott and it looks like they have a four wheeler on the back of the truck. Let's go out to the carriage house and take a look," Megan said.

Elana was anxious to go out to the carriage house so she could look around and was glad all of them would be there. She didn't want to go alone. She and Megan went out the kitchen door and met the guys at the front of the carriage house. Elana's necklace started to vibrate but it only lasted a few seconds. She was sure Scott's was vibrating too because he got a strange look on his face and his hand went to the necklace.

Scott looked at her questioningly and she nodded that she knew what he was wondering. He grinned and went to help Darren unload the four wheeler.

"She's a beaut don't you think," Scott said to Elana.

"Sure is and you have lots of room to ride it. Just don't get lost."

"I was a boy scout I'll have you know and we don't get lost."

"Yeah, sure," Elana teased.

"Grab yours and we'll park them in front of the house while we eat lunch and then we'll take a ride. You girls want to tag along?" Scott asked.

"No, we have some exploring to do ourselves," Elana said.

They made sandwiches and a salad for lunch. Elana filled them in on the hidden rooms.

"Megan and I are going to try to find the rooms in both houses today and if there's time, we might look in the old school."

"If you find hidden treasure, we get to share it," Scott told her and Megan, "If you find dead bodies, you can keep them."

"No telling what we'll find, hopefully it's interesting," Elana mused.

"We'll be back well before dark," Scott told the girls. We're going to ride over to the right behind the barn

180

today and then explore the other side of the grounds tomorrow if the weather's good."

"Have fun and be careful. You don't know what might be out there," Elana cautioned.

"Better not run across any more bodies," Darren said seriously.

"I certainly hope you don't," Megan said.

The guys started up their four wheelers and took off towards the barn both riding cautiously which impressed both Megan and Elana.

"Once they get the feel of those things, they'll drive like maniacs but right now, they seem to be trying to drive careful," Elana observed.

"Yeah, just a couple of little boys playing," Megan laughed.

"Let's put the dishes in the sink and try to find those hidden rooms," Elana said.

"I don't even know where to start but I imagine they are in the main part of the house."

"Me too. I pushed on all the walls here in the kitchen and none of them moved so let's start with the dining room. I wonder how big the room will be."

Chapter 18

Elana and Megan walked into each room on the first floor and tried to imagine where a room might be hidden. All of the outside walls had windows or doors so they knew it couldn't be on an outside wall.

When they entered the study, behind the parlor, they noticed there were no doors or windows on the back wall. The wall was paneled so they pushed each panel to see if it miraculously turned into a door. No such luck.

"Well, that's about the only place a hidden room could be downstairs," Elana remarked.

"It has to be here. A room upstairs makes no sense because if they had to run and hide, it would take too long to run up the stairs. Maybe the entrance is in the foyer or the hallway," Megan offered.

"Let's go see."

They went to the back of the foyer to look around. The wainscoting had medallions placed every twenty four or so inches so she tried turning each one. They were difficult to turn but all at once, viola, a door creaked open. It was a small door and difficult to open all the way.

"We found it!" Elana squealed. "I wonder if any of the other owners found this room. I would have thought Cory and his wife would know it's here since they remodeled.

"Oh, it's dusty in there. I'll bet no one has been in there for years," Megan said.

They started to walk through the opening when Elana said, "wait a minute."

She went to the kitchen and brought back a chair. "Let's prop the door open with this so we won't get locked in there. I brought a couple of flashlights too, it's pretty dark."

"Good idea," Megan said. "I'm sure the guys would let us out but I don't like small places."

They propped the door open and cautiously walked into the room. Cobwebs and dust was everywhere.

"Ewww, I hate spiders," Megan screamed as she brushed her hair and shoulders. "Do I have one on me?"

"No, just some cobwebs. I think the spiders gave up long ago," Elana laughed.

"Doesn't seem to be anything in here except for the candlesticks on that table over there," Megan observed.

Elana shined her flashlight over to the table and noticed an old book beside the candle sticks.

"Wonder if that's another journal. Hope so."

They walked closer and saw the book was an old bible. Elana opened it and read the inscription on the inside: *Caleb Ashbey and Isabella Sanders Married June 9, 1866* and below that *Lillian Mae September 2 1867 Joseph David September 10 1869.*

"Look at this beautiful handwriting. This must be the people who built the house's bible. I'll bet they forgot it when they moved. I wonder why it was in this room though," Elana said. "Looks like they had two children. I wonder what became of them."

"Maybe they put it in here for something to pass the time in case they were in here for a long time. Elana, wasn't your great grandmother an Ashbey?" Megan asked.

"Yes, I think Mom traced the family and did say something about someone being named Ashbey. I wonder if I'm related to this bunch. Let's take it out in the light to see if there is anything interesting in it, and I'm going to call Mom. I didn't even think about maybe being related to Captain Ashbey."

"Hello, Mom, it's me," Elana said when her mother answered the phone.

"Hi dear, is everything all right?" her mother inquired since she seldom heard from her daughter unless there was something wrong.

"No, everything is great, just have a question. Did you say we were related to people named Ashbey?"

"Yes, your grandmother's maternal side had some Ashbeys on it. I was just working on this so let me see," she said as she leafed through some papers. "Yes, there is a Lillian Ashbey and her mother was Isabella. Why do you ask?"

"What relation would they be to me?"

"Your grandmothers, why?" her mother asked impatiently.

"You're never gonna believe this but Scott and I just bought a plantation that was built by Isabella and her husband. Lillian was born here."

"Get outta here, no way," her mother exclaimed.

"Yes and we just found Isabella's old bible and, did you know Isabella ran a whore house out here during the Civil War?"

"I sure didn't. In the house you bought?"

"No, there's a really old stone building on the property and that's where the whore house was."

"Oh, I've got to come out to visit. Okay if I come out any time?"

"Sure, we have plenty of room for you to stay as long as you want."

"Fantastic, I'll let you know when to expect me. Scott won't mind will he?"

"Heavens no, he loves you."

"Okay, be talking to you soon. Bye."

"Bye"

"Mom's coming to visit," Elana told Megan. "She's real excited about our find since she's been tracing our family for years."

They took the bible to the kitchen and dusted it off and carefully opened it. It was full of notes, letters and pictures. One note stood out to Elana.

I wish Essie hadn't killed those outlaws. Evil men turn into evil spirits. It's been 4 years since that awful day and its evident there are evil spirits just waiting to be released. The ground at the hog pen shakes sometime every August for no real reason other than the evil spirits trying to escape. Heaven help us if they ever do. Sarah sprinkles hog's blood in that fateful corner of the hog pen every full moon to ward off the spirits. So far, nothing has happened but I'm always frightened during August.

"What's that?" Megan asks.

"It's a note the woman who lived in the house wrote about someone killing outlaws."

"Let me see," Megan said taking the note.

Megan read the note and asked, "Where do you suppose the hog pen was?"

"According to Lucy's journal, it was behind the carriage house."

"Do you think this has anything to do with the strange things that have happened around here?" Megan asked.

"I'm not sure but Jett, the real estate agent had the accident in August and from what I remember, the body that Darren found in the car was here at an open house around the same time last year. A lot of coincidences here. I wonder when Mr. Jenkins' mother-in-law got sick."

"Let's call Debra at the real estate office and see if she knows," Megan suggested.

"Good idea," Elana said as she dialed the number. "Hi, can I speak to Debra?" She asked the receptionist.

"Sure, who can I say is calling?"

"This is Elana Palmer."

"Thanks, Elana, just a second."

"Hello, Elana, is everything alright?" Debra inquired.

"Just wonderful but I have a question. Do you happen to know when Mr. Jenkins' mother-in-law got sick out here at the plantation?"

"Let me see if there's anything in his file to indicate that. Yes, it says here that she got sick in August 2007."

"And she died right after that same month, correct?" Elana asked.

"That's right."

"Thanks so much, Debra," Elana said.

"Is there anything else I can do for you?" Debra asked.

"No, nice talking to you, bye." And Elana hung up.

"You're white as a sheet," Megan replied.

"This is too strange. Both real estate agents died in August, Mr. Jenkins' mother-in-law got sick here in August 2007 and died later that month. A lot of strange things happening in August around here. Sure glad it's September."

"Wow, let's plan to take vacations in August," Megan said jokingly but really meant it.

"I say we get to the bottom of this. No spirits, evil or not are going to run me off my land," Elana stated. "It says here that Sarah sprinkled hogs blood around at the full moon each August so maybe we can do the same."

"Where are we going to get hogs blood and how do we know where to sprinkle it?" Megan asked.

"I'm sure the slaughterhouse down the road will save us some. Might think we're crazy but I don't care about that and we'll find out for sure where the hog pen was."

"I'm game if you are but I don't want any spirits killing us."

"Me neither if I can help it."

"We need to talk to Darren and Scott and let them know what we've found out," Megan said.

"Do you think Darren will still want to live here?" Elana asked.

"Oh yeah, he loves a good mystery and the scarier the better but he'll never believe in evil spirits."

"Want to go over to the small house to see if we can find the room over there?" Elana asked Megan.

"Sure. Let's take the chair and flashlights though."

They walked over to the other house and let themselves in the front door. They looked around and didn't see any place where there might be a hidden room.

"I'll bet the hidden room is between the front room and the kitchen," Megan offered. "It looks like the wainscoting has the same medallions as the big house. Let's check it out and see if any of them move."

They walked to the back of the front room under the stairway and began turning each medallion until one gave just a little.

189

"I think this is it," Elana said as a door creaked open. "Bring the chair over and we'll have a look."

Elana propped the door open with the chair as Megan shined the light into the little room. This room was just as dusty as the other one. There were two trunks in the room and both Megan and Elana were eager to see what was inside. When they got inside the room, they noticed a small cradle behind one of the trunks.

They carefully opened the first trunk and saw it was about half full of clothing. The clothing appeared to belong to babies and small children and was very old fashioned.

"I'll bet this is clothing worn by the children of the woman who lived here long ago," Megan said. "It's strange she didn't take these things with her when they moved."

"Yes, she mentioned that she came in here and sat among her baby's things from time to time. I'll bet the other trunk has her husband's clothing because she also said she sat among his things."

"Let's open it and see," Megan said. "I hope we don't release any ghosts though. This looks like the perfect place for a ghost to live."

They carefully opened the other trunk and sure enough it was about half full of men's clothing. On top was an old straw hat that had seen its better days. At the bottom of the trunk was a beautiful dress.

"I wonder if this was her wedding dress." Elana said.

"It's beautiful!" Megan exclaimed.

"I wonder if this cradle belonged to her children." Elana said as she touched the cradle.

"I'm sure it did. It probably held each of them. I can just imagine her sitting beside it and rocking her babies to sleep," Megan said as she also touched the cradle.

"I'm going to ask Scott's boss if he wants these things unless you want them. I don't have any use for them."

"Good idea. I don't want them. I want to use this room for storage or maybe a powder room and they should be with their rightful family."

"I think I hear Scott and Darren's four wheelers," Elana said as she started towards the door. "Let's lock up and see what they found. Hope they found something interesting too."

Megan and Elana met the guys at the carriage house just as Darren was opening the door to put the four wheelers away. Scott drove his ATV into the garage with Darren following.

"You'll never guess what we found out there," Darren said.

"Not another body or wrecked car, I hope," Megan said.

"No, but something better," Scott offered.

"What?" Elana asked.

"We found two cemeteries, an apple orchard and an old stone building," Darren piped in. "And we haven't even touched most of the property. There's a wealth of history here."

"How old are the cemeteries?" Elana asked.

"One had a date in the late 1800s and the other the early 1800s. Not sure about the names. They were pretty deteriorated and we didn't take time to really look that close. Both were all grown up and truthfully, I was afraid of snakes," Darren admitted.

"Maybe we can go back when the weather gets cold and clean them up a bit and see if we can see the names," Megan offered.

"That would be fun," Elana said. "I'm sure some of the graves belong to the woman who wrote the journal. The older ones could be from when the old school was a church and preacher's house."

"So what did you girls find?" Darren asked.

"We found the hidden room in each of the houses. There was an old bible and some candle holders in the big house and two trunks of clothes in the little house. Both rooms looked like they had been closed up for years," Elana said.

"Wonder who the stuff belonged to?" Scott asked.

"I think the bible belonged to the couple that built the house. It had her name and her husband's name along with their date of marriage and children's births. The clothes in the little house appear to have belonged to the babies and husband of the woman who lived there at the same time. Oh and there was a beautiful dress in one of the trunks that could be an old wedding dress," Megan said.

"Scott, do you think Stan would like the trunks? I'm sure they belonged to his grandmother," Elana asked. "I don't want them and it would be a shame to put them in the trash."

"I'll ask him but I'm pretty sure he will."

"We can give them to him at the dinner party," Elana said. "I'm planning it for a week from Saturday so be sure to remind him and of the date and time."

"Okay," Scott said. "But you'll have to remind me Monday morning. Let's drive into town and grab some dinner and maybe a movie."

"All right, let's get ready and meet in the foyer in an hour," Megan said as she and Darren started back to the house.

"Scott, I need to talk to you," Elana said nervously.

"I need to talk to you too," Scott replied with a very serious look on his face.

She told him all she had read about the hog pen, the carriage house and the spirits. "Every time I come near the carriage house, my necklace vibrates," she said.

"That's what I wanted to talk to you about, mine vibrates too."

"I think there might be something to the spirits and the deaths that have happened," Elana said seriously. "Too many coincidences."

"What are we going to do? We can't just up and move," Scott said.

"Oh I don't want to move, I love it here. I want to get rid of the spirits," Elana said.

"I'm all for that but how can we do it?"

"I'm not real sure but from what I've read, we have until next August to figure it out." Elana said hoping they actually did have until next August.

"We can discuss this later then. Let's get back to the house and get ready for dinner, I'm starved and in need of some serious relaxation," Scott said as he locked the carriage house door.

Chapter 19

Elana and Megan sat on the porch waiting for the furniture to be delivered. They had spent the last two days cleaning, scrubbing and waxing the entire house in preparation for the furniture. Once everything was in place, they were going to go shopping for accessories.

"I think we will need area rugs, window treatments, knickknacks, picture frames, and anything else we think will make this place a home," Elana said.

"You can pick out stuff for the house but I want to pick out for our rooms over the kitchen," Megan told her.

"Oh, you bet. I wouldn't even want to begin to figure out what you and Darren like but I do want you to have a say in the rest of the house. After all, you will be living there as much as we will. I'll pick out things for the other bedrooms though."

"I think I hear the truck coming," Megan said. "I can't wait to see how the new furniture will look."

"Yeah, I can see the dust. I think we need to pave the driveway next spring to cut down on all that dust."

The truck pulled up to the front of the house and two men climbed out.

"Hi, I'm Jess and this is Tony. We loaded the truck with bedroom furniture on the back and the living room furniture to the front. Want to show us where the stuff is to go?" Jess asked.

"Some of it goes in this part of the house and the rest goes in the rooms over the kitchen in the back. It'll be easier to take that furniture in the back way."

"Okay, we'll set it out and you all can tell us where it goes. If it goes in the back, we can reload and drive back there after the rest of the furniture's inside," the driver said as they started unloading the truck.

"Sounds good," Megan said.

They unloaded a king size bed frame, mattress and springs, two night stands, two dressers, a vanity, a sofa, two easy chairs and a couple of end tables first.

"Oh, those all go above the kitchen. There should be a coffee table and a TV stand someplace too," Megan offered.

"OK, just tell us which ones they are and we'll leave them all here until later," Tony said.

Both guys were tanned and muscular and very personable. They worked fast and were very careful with all the furniture.

"I think we delivered furniture out here a few years ago," Jess said as he looked around.

"You might have. The previous owners did a lot of work and decorating when they moved in," Elana said.

"Why did they move, this is a beautiful house?" Tony asked.

"The man's mother-in-law didn't like it here so his wife decided she wanted to move, go figure," Elana laughed.

The guys unloaded the dining room furniture and Elana and Megan directed them to the dining room.

"Just place it anywhere, we'll have our husbands arrange the rooms to suit us," Elana told them as they carried the sideboard into the dining room.

"We don't mind placing the things in the general direction if you want," Jess said.

"That would be fantastic, put that piece against the outside wall and the other sideboard will go on the inside wall. Put the table in the center," Elana instructed.

When the furniture had been placed in the dining room, they started to unload the living room furniture. Elana told them to just place that furniture in the room and they would decide later how to arrange it.

"The bedroom furniture goes upstairs," Elana said as she pointed to the stairs. "That bed goes in the room to the right at the top of the stairs. The other beds go in any of the other bedrooms to the left."

When all the beds had been carried up stairs, they unloaded the dressers, night stands, and bureaus. Elana instructed them on which room to place each piece.

"You don't have to arrange the bedrooms, just put the furniture in them and we'll take care of the rest."

"Can we get you a soda or something?" Megan asked. You must be thirsty after all that hard work in the sun."

"A soda would be great, it sure is hot here," both guys said at once.

Megan went inside and returned with sodas for everyone. The men sat on the steps while they emptied their cans.

"This is sure beautiful out here. What is the old stone building?" Tony asked.

"It used to be a school for women, before that a brothel during the Civil War and a Glebe house before that," Elana said.

"Wow, a brothel during the Civil War, that's interesting," Tony laughed.

"We're going to open a couples retreat in a year or so in it," Megan said.

"That's a good idea," Jess said as he got up and headed for the truck. "Let's get back to work."

They loaded the furniture for over the kitchen back into the truck and followed Elana and Megan to the back entrance.

Elana unlocked the door and showed them where the stairs were.

"Let's carry some of the furniture into the kitchen and then carry it on upstairs. There's plenty of room for most of it," Tony said as he looked around the room.

When all the furniture was upstairs, Tony and Jess thanked Megan and Elana and started back to their truck.

"Hey guys, wait up," Elana said as she reached for her purse. "Here ya go," she said as she handed each of them a fifty dollar bill.

"Aw, you don't have to do that," Jess said.

"Worth every penny," Elana told them.

"Gee, thanks!" both said with a huge grin.

The guys got into the truck and drove around the house to the driveway. They hadn't been gone more than twenty minutes when Scott and Darren got home.

"Furniture was delivered today," Megan said as they each got out of their cars.

"Guess we'll be busy this evening," Darren complained. "I was planning to relax and watch some TV."

"No, we have most of the important furniture placed where we want it. Just have to make up the beds if you want to help with that after supper," Elana told them.

"We'll pass," Scott laughed.

"What's for supper, I'm starved," Darren said as he walked up the steps to the front porch.

"I think I'll order pizza if that's okay," Elana said.

"Sounds good," Scott said.

Elana called in the pizza order and they went into the living room to admire the new furniture even though the room still looked bare.

When the pizza arrived, Elana instructed them to sit on the old sofa and chairs to eat. "I don't want pizza on the new furniture, at least not tonight," she laughed.

After they ate, Megan and Elana carried the dishes to the kitchen and put them in the dishwasher. They went back into the dining room and talked about how to arrange that room for the dinner party.

"We better get the beds made up," Megan suggested.

"I'll help you and then you can help me," Elana said. "Oh, let me lock the kitchen door first."

"Glad you thought about that, I would have forgotten. We need to get a system in place for making sure everything is locked up when we aren't in here or the rest of the house," Megan said.

"Yeah, someone could slip into the house and we'd never know but I don't think we need to check the windows unless we open them."

"I can't wait for Mom to come visit," Elana said as they were making up the bed in Megan and Darren's room.

"Your mother is such a sweet lady, I'm anxious to see her again. She's never met Darren but I think they will get along fabulously. What do you think?"

"Oh they will but Mom will flirt up a storm. Gotta watch her around young guys. She can be a cougar."

"That's funny. Darren will eat that up."

"This little apartment looks so cozy," Elana said as she walked into the room they set up as a living room."

"It is, I just love it. I do so appreciate you letting us live here," Megan said.

"I'm the one who appreciates you all agreeing to live here. I'd be beside myself out here all alone when Scott is away."

"It would be kind of lonesome and a bit scary."

"I'm not really scared, just uncomfortable at times. I think it's mostly because I'm not used to the place. I was uncomfortable at our old apartment until I got used to it."

"All done here, let's get your bed made up and then relax for a bit," Megan said.

When they had finished upstairs, Megan and Elana went down and found the guys sitting on the front porch drinking a beer. The front porch is one of the things Elana loved about this place.

"We were just wondering how we should go about remodeling the little house. We want to do most of the work ourselves but we're not sure where to start," Darren said.

"Maybe you could draw up the plans for how you want it to look and hire a contractor to do the heavy work and then you all do the finishing," Elana suggested.

"Good idea," Scott said.

"Sure is. Takes a load off my mind. We can draw up plans pretty easy but turning those plans into a finished project is tough," Darren said.

"Be quicker to have a contractor do the work too," Megan laughed. They can be in here and back out while you all are still getting the tools set up.

Darren swatted her backside and said, "No confidence at all in our expertise."

"Nope, I know you both and contractors you aren't.

"I agree with that," Elana laughed. "Got any more of those beers?"

"In the cooler over there," Scott said. "Have to carry a cooler around here because it's so far to the kitchen."

"Oh, Mom is coming to visit. I told her about the house belonging to our relatives and she wants to see it," Elana said.

"What do you mean, belonged to our relatives?" Scott asked.

"Didn't I tell you, we found a bible and it seems that the woman who ran the whore house and later built this house is my great, great, great grandmother."

"No shit, that's something. Wait till I tell Stan," Scott said. "He's going to be so excited. He's always talking about his ancestors. I don't know why he doesn't pay someone to research his family.

"We can tell him at the dinner party next Saturday.

"Unbelievable," Darren said. "What's the chances of buying a plantation that belonged to you own family? Looks like you could have just inherited it."

"Maybe we did a long time ago," Elana said. "I think I was destined to find this place and buy it. I still can't believe I just ran across it that day I was driving around."

"Luck or karma," Megan said.

"I think I have a mission to carry out here, just don't know yet what it is."

"Listen," Megan said as she turned her ear to the field. "Hear the night sounds. So peaceful. Not like the sounds in the city. Horns blasting, sirens wailing, kids screaming. So peaceful I could sit here listening for hours."

"It is peaceful. We need to build a patio out back with a fire pit and barbeque grill for summer parties," Scott said.

"Let's plan to do that this spring so we can have a proper house warming party," Elana suggested.

"We can have a dual house warming party," Megan laughed. "Our house and yours."

"Fantastic idea," Elana agreed.

Elana's cell phone started ringing as she was getting a beer from the cooler. "Hello," she said not looking at the caller ID.

"Hi sweetie, is it okay if I come up this weekend and stay for a couple of weeks?" her mother asked, Her mother had retired to Tampa just after her father died three years ago and hadn't been back north since.

"Of course, I'd love you to stay a month!"

"Can't stay away that long, but two weeks will work fine."

"Great, let me know when to pick you up and which airport," Elana told her.

"Will do. Talk to you later."

"That was Mom, she's coming this weekend for two weeks," Elana told everyone. "I want to get her room fixed up before she gets here. I wonder if I can postpone starting my internship until after she leaves."

"I'm sure you can, after all, it's not a paid position," Megan said.

"I'll call tomorrow to make sure. I don't want Mom out here all alone. Don't tell her I'm postponing my start date or she'll be upset."

"We won't say a word," all agreed.

Elana sat down and leaned back against Scott's chest. "I could sit here all night but I think we probably should get to bed. We both have to get up early."

"Yeah, I'm beat and I have to be at work early in the morning. There's a big meeting with all the executives and I don't want to be late since this is my first meeting," Scott said.

"Let's call it a night," Darren said getting up and helping Megan to her feet.

"Okay, be sure to check the lock on the kitchen door," Elana reminded them.

"I thought you checked it earlier," Megan said.

"Check it again. I want you to get in the habit of checking it every evening before going up stairs."

"Okay, worry wart," Darren said with a chuckle.

Chapter *20*

That night Elana had a nightmare. The first one she had since she was a teenager at her parent's house. She woke screaming and shaking but couldn't remember the dream.

"Easy baby, it was only a dream," Scott comforted her while cradling her in his arms. "I'm here with you."

"It was terrible but I can't seem to remember it," she wailed as flashes of the dream went through her mind.

"Just sit quietly for a few minutes and calm down. I'm right here."

After about ten minutes, she had calmed down enough to try to go back to sleep. She slept fitfully the rest of the night but the dream recurred throughout the night. Each time she woke, she could only remember bits and pieces.

Scott got up the next morning and tried to not awaken Elana but she started stirring as soon as he got out of bed.

"Is it time to get up?" she asked.

"No, stay in bed. I can grab something to eat on the way to work."

"I think I will, I'm beat. See you this evening."

"Sleep tight," he said as he bent down and kissed her forehead. He thought she felt warm but decided it was just because she was bundled up in the covers.

After a while, Elana dragged herself out of bed and jumped in the shower. She began to feel almost human as she was drying herself and getting dressed.

I sure hope I sleep better tonight, she thought to herself as she walked downstairs to the kitchen.

Megan had left some oatmeal and bacon on the stove so Elana made a quick breakfast and cleared the breakfast mess before getting ready to drive down to Dr. Meadow's office. She was reluctant to ask if she could postpone her internship start date for a couple of weeks but didn't feel comfortable leaving her mother alone.

Elana walked up to the receptionist desk at Dr. Meadow's office and said, "Hi, I'm Elana Palmer. I'm supposed to start my internship the first of the week and wonder if I can postpone it for two weeks."

"Hi Elana, let me check," the receptionist said. "Dr. Meadows, would it be possible for Elana to start her internship in two weeks instead of the first of next week?"

"Is she here?" Dr. Meadows asked.

"Yes."

"Send her into my office. I have her orientation material here."

"Elana, Dr. Meadows would like to talk to you."

"Is he upset?" Elana asked.

"Oh no, he's very easy going," the receptionist. "I think he just wants to go over some of the orientation with you. His door is right over there."

"Thanks," Elana said as she walked towards the door.

Just then the door opened and Dr. Meadows smiled and said, "Good morning Elana, come on in."

"I'm so sorry to make this request, Dr. Meadows. It's just that my mother is making a surprise visit and I haven't seen her for over a year."

"No problem but you don't have to postpone your internship, you can work on the first couple of weeks at home. It's just orientation and everything is on the computer. You do have Internet access at home?"

"Yes, of course. Thank you so much."

"I'll just get the paper work for your security access and you can take it to IT and they will get you all set up."

"Wonderful."

"Here you are, just take these downstairs to IT and anyone there can help you. If you have any problems with your orientation, just email me and I'll be happy to help you," Dr. Meadows told her as he handed her the paperwork.

"Thanks again Dr. Meadows."

She took the elevator down to the lower floor and followed the signs to the IT department.

She walked into the reception area and introduced herself.

"Oh, yes, Dr. Meadows just called down and told me to expect you. I'll just be a few minutes setting up your security access to the network. You can sit over there if you want. It won't take long."

"Thanks," Elana said as she took a seat on the sofa.

After about ten minutes, the girl at the desk motioned her over. "Here's your username, password and security access code. The web address is right here," she said as she pointed to a line on the paper. "Once you're at our web site, follow the directions on the sheet to download the connection software and if you have any problems at all, call this number for help. Once you are in the system, you'll find all the material you need for your orientation. You can work on it at your leisure as long as you complete each requirement by the appropriate date. You can print out the handbook if you want or just read it online. Do you have any questions?"

"No questions yet, this is super," Elana said as she took the small packet of papers. She was sure she wouldn't have any problems getting connected but was glad there was help just in case.

"Dr. Meadows' secretary will send you an email once you complete orientation giving you your schedule and job duties."

"Thank you so much," Elana said as she left the IT department and headed for the door.

This is going to be fantastic. I can work and still spend time with Mom.

Her phone rang just as she was getting into her car. It was her mother.

"Hi Mom, what's up?" she asked.

"Oh nothing much except that I could only get a flight for Friday instead of Saturday if that's okay with you."

"No problem, we'll just have more time to spend together."

"I'll email my itinerary and you can pick me up at the airport or I can take a taxi."

"I can pick you up. I don't have to go in for my internship until after your visit. The doctor has made arrangements for me to do my two week orientation online at home."

"I hope I'm not putting you out or causing you problems with your job."

"Mom, I haven't seen you in over a year. Nothing is more important than your visit right now. I'm so anxious to see you and to have you see our new place. Besides, it isn't really a job, it's an internship."

"Okay, it's settled, I'll see you Friday."

"Bye Mom, I'm on my way home now. Call again this evening if you want."

"I just might, bye."

Elana stopped by the market to pick up the makings for spaghetti for dinner. Next she went to Chips and Chowder and confirmed the menu and plans for the dinner party and then drove home. She was glad to see that Megan was already there so she could help with dinner.

Elana let herself in the kitchen door and put the groceries on the counter and started preparing dinner. "Megan, I'm in the kitchen," she called.

When Megan didn't reply, she wandered around the house trying to find her. She called again, "Megan, are you here?"

Still no answer. Now she was getting worried. It wasn't like Megan to not answer. Elana went up stairs to the apartment over the kitchen but Megan wasn't there either.

"Wonder where she could be?" she thought as she went outside.

She looked all around the back yard and down to the carriage house but saw no sign of her. Then she looked over at the small house and saw Megan coming out the door.

"There you are," Elana shouted. "I thought you were lost."

"No, I was just looking over the rooms. Darren and I are going to draw up some plans for the contractor and I wanted to take another look. It is such a cute little place and will look wonderful. I think we can make it into a cozy little home for us."

"I'm going to call the water department and power company tomorrow to schedule installation of water and electricity. I think I'll have them put in the lines to the old school while they're here," Elana said.

"Seems like there's a lot to be done but we'll get there," Megan said. "I'm anxious to get started so we can move in."

"Just hope we don't forget anything with winter coming," Elana told her. "Oh, I got stuff for spaghetti for dinner. The noodles are already in the pot."

"Fantastic, I'll finish it up if you want."

"We can work together. I don't have any plans until after dinner."

After the table had been cleared and the dishes put in the dishwasher, Elana decided to try to get online with Dr. Meadow's office. It took about an hour to download the connection and get everything working but she was ready to start the next morning. She figured she could get a good bit done before picking her mother up at the airport.

Later that evening, Megan motioned Elana to come to the kitchen with her.

"What's up Megan?" Elana asked.

"I'm not sure where to begin but have you felt things just aren't quite right around here?"

"How so," Elana asked trying to be nonchalant.

"Well, the carriage house for one thing, it just seems to feel weird out there and Darren has noticed it too. I felt this even before you told me about the journal entry. Then today, as I was leaving the house, I saw an old woman in the yard. She just stood there smiling at me and then disappeared. I'm not afraid of ghosts, hell I don't even think I believe in them but there's something," Megan said.

"Since you're asking, yes there is something weird about this place. Scott and I both feel it at the carriage house. I feel it has something to do with the hog pen that used to be there. As for the old woman, I've seen her too and I think she is friendly. Just stay away from the carriage house or take someone with you if you have to go down there until I know more," Elana told her.

"Thanks, I think it makes me feel better that you feel the same. I'm not even considering leaving here but I would like to know what's going on."

"You and me both and I aim to find out. Want to help me?"

"You know I do. I love a good mystery but sure don't want to get hurt or killed.

"What's this a hen party," Scott said as he walked into the kitchen, concerned at both women's serious look.

"Sort of, we're discussing the weird things that have been happening around here," Elana said.

"Oh yeah, lots of strange things but it's an old place with lots of history. What time's your mother getting in tomorrow?"

"I'm picking her up at three so we should be home by dinner time. Let's take her out for dinner instead of trying to cook, okay?"

"Okay by me, how about you and Darren," Scott asked Megan.

"Sure."

"How about the Blue Goose?" Scott asked "It's a great place to eat."

"Sounds good," Elana replied.

"I'll call in the reservation. How's seven tomorrow evening work?"

"We should be able to make that," both women said.

"I forgot to tell you, Stan's dad is in town so I told him it was okay to bring him Saturday evening," Scott told Elana.

"Wonderful, I was trying to think of someone to invite for Mom to sit with and this will be perfect. You know she'll scold you for trying to fix her up don't you?" she laughed.

"Well, maybe they'll hit it off. Stan's mother passed about the same time as your dad."

"We can hope. How long is he in town?"

"I think until next weekend."

"Maybe if he and Mom hit it off, he can take her off my hands for a while each day so I can work," Elana said.

"By the way, what are we having Saturday?" Scott asked.

"They'll set up hors d'oeuvres and drinks before dinner. For dinner we chose surf and turf. We'll start with clam chowder or vegetable soup and house salad, then prime rib and lobster tails with a vegetable and their house chips. We'll wrap it up with key lime pie or coconut cream. They'll be bringing some bottles of their best wine too," Elana reported. "I think we've covered everything and the menu should appeal to everyone's taste."

"Sounds delicious," Scott said.

"Sure does," Darren chimed in.

Elana decided to spend the morning working on her internship and then taking care of chores before picking her mother up in the afternoon. She read through most of the user manual and answered the questions in section one and turned those in. She would work some more later tonight after everyone had gone to bed so she wouldn't get behind.

After lunch, she drove to the water department and then the power company to set up the installations. She just had time to get to the airport as her mother's plane was landing. She was so anxious to see her mother again.

She met her mother, Kathy, and after picking up her luggage, drove back to the house. They talked nonstop all the way. Kathy was in her late fifties but looked much younger. Her blond hair was cut in a style that framed her thin face and camouflaged what few wrinkles she had. She had put on a few pounds since her husband Kendal died but in the right places. She had a deep tan and wore a flowered blouse and white capris that fit just right.

"Mom you look wonderful," Elana told her. "Life in Florida is sure agreeing with you."

"I love it there but do miss spending time with you."

"Maybe you can summer with us now that we have all this room."

"That would be terrific. It does get hot down there in the summer."

"We can fix up a room or two just for you to use anytime you want."

"I'll really think about it."

"Here we are," Elana said as they turned into the driveway."

As they drove up to the house Kathy let out a squeal. "This is fantastic! I didn't even imagine how beautiful it would be."

"It is beautiful. I'm anxious to show you around but that will have to wait until tomorrow. We have reservations at the Blue Goose and we'll just have enough time to get ready and get there."

"Tomorrow is plenty soon enough but I do want to see that bible tonight."

"Remind me when we get back from dinner. You're welcome to take it to your room and look it over if you want."

Chapter 21

Scott and Darren spent Saturday morning going over the plans for the house renovation. They wanted to be sure they had thought of everything before turning it over to the contractor. Once the contractor started working, it might be difficult to make changes. They would need plumbing and wiring installed. They were going to have a full bath built upstairs and a half bath down along with a built in kitchen dining room combination. The house was small but if they remodeled it right, it would be plenty big enough for Darren and Megan until they decided to buy their own home or build on to this one.

Elana and Megan gave Kathy the grand tour of the small house and then the mansion.

"Megan and Darren are going to live in the small house and help us with the property. When we get the couples retreat operational, Megan will partner with me to run it," Elana told her mother. "I haven't mentioned to her or

Darren yet but I've been thinking they could buy a few acres from us and build their own house later on."

"Elana, that's a great idea," Megan squealed.

They took Kathy through the entire mansion stopping at each room to go into detail about the future plans for decorating. When they got to the parlor and study Elana told her mother that this was where she planned on setting up an office for both her and Megan for counseling couples until the old school building was remodeled.

Kathy was making mental notes about suggestions she had for each room. She practiced Feng Shui and loved decorating.

"I think it will probably take a couple of years to get the building in shape and I want us to start our practice as soon as we're through with our internship."

"These rooms will make perfect offices for you and maybe the small sunroom off the parlor could serve as a reception area. Keep me in mind if you need a receptionist," Kathy teased.

"Would you work for us?" Elana asked.

"Depends, how much you plan to pay?" Kathy laughed. "You haven't shown me the school or the carriage house, let's go take a look at those before we have to start getting ready for dinner."

"OK, let's look at the school first," Elana offered.

They walked up onto the porch and peeked in the door. "My goodness, look at that staircase," Kathy exclaimed.

"Please tell me you are going to renovate that and not tear it out. That staircase is priceless."

"Yes, that stays. Maybe when we get ready to plan out the retreat you can come up and give us some suggestions. Aren't you a Feng Shui enthusiast?"

"I sure am and I'd be delighted to give some opinions here and in the house."

"Want to go inside? This place is awesome."

"I thought you weren't going to ask."

They walked around the downstairs and then up the stairway to the rooms above.

"Dear, this is a lovely old building and I can see that it must have been an elegant brothel in its time."

"Oh dear, look at the time," Elana said as she looked at her watch. "We'll have to look at the carriage house another day, it's almost 3:30 and the caterers will be here in an hour or so. It's just an old garage with a couple of storage rooms. Darren and Scott are going to make it into a man cave once the little house is done."

"I don't need to see a garage," Kathy said much to Elana's relief. She wasn't ready for her mother's questions if she too felt the weird feelings out there.

The caterers from Chips and Chowder parked near the kitchen door and started carrying in all the food and equipment they would need for the dinner party. They would provide everything, even the china and silverware. The waiter and waitress were dressed in black pants and white shirt and the other staff was all in white.

Shortly after 5:00 Stan, his wife and his dad arrived. Elana was surprised to see that Stan's dad was gorgeous. She knew her mother would be impressed. She just hoped he wasn't stuck on himself. It seemed to her that most attractive older men were conceited.

"Come in," Scott said as he opened the door. "Everyone is in the living room."

"Everyone, this is my boss Stan, his wife Connie and his dad Isaac. This is my wife Elana," Scott said as he gave Elana a gentle hug. That's Megan and Darren over there," Scott said pointing to the couch across the room. "And this is Elana's mother, Kathy," he said placing an arm around her shoulder.

Pleasantries were exchanged and Scott asked, "Would you like to see the house where your grandparents lived?"

"That's one of the reasons we're here," Stan said. "I was telling dad about it and he's excited to see it. He was named after their son who would be a grandfather too."

"I think I'll stay here," Megan said.

"Me too, I saw the house a little bit ago," Elana's mother said.

"Let's go, it's not far."

"Is that the house?" Stan asked as they neared the house.

"Sure is. I don't think anyone has lived there since your grandparents and there are two trunks and an old cradle in a hidden room that you can have if you want them," Scott said.

220

"Yes, we want them. Is there anything in the trunks?" Isaac asked.

"As a matter of fact there's a lot of old clothing in them," Elana said.

They showed Stan, his wife and dad the house and then opened the hidden room. Stan almost had tears in his eyes as he looked at the clothing in each of the trunks. "Kind of makes me emotional to see things that belonged to relatives so long ago."

"I read Lucy's journal and I think you'll be interested in some of the things she had to say," Elana told him.

"Oh yes, I want to know everything. I really need to read it myself."

"I think you would be impressed once you got used to the writing."

"You can pick up the trunks and cradle anytime you want," Scott told Stan. "And you can take the journal with you tonight if you want."

"Are you sure you're through with it, Elana?" Stan asked.

"I'd like to keep it a bit longer but you should have it now."

"Why don't you hold onto it until you're sure you're through with it then?"

"Thanks, I will. I'd really like to read it again to make sure I haven't missed anything."

The waiter and waitress served hors d'oeuvres and drinks while they were waiting for dinner to be served.

Isaac sat down on the sofa beside Elana's mother. "The kids have a pretty special place here."

"Yes, and it was built by my family. I'm not sure if you know the story or not but the woman who originally lived here had a brothel in the old stone building."

"I did know that and, my great, great, great grandmother worked for her.

"I knew that too. Seems we have very colorful family skeletons."

"I think I need to hire a genealogist to trace my remarkable family tree," Isaac said.

"Look no further, I do genealogy and would love to help you."

"You're hired! Seems like we are almost kin folk anyway," Isaac laughed.

"Looks like your dad and Elana's mom are hitting it off," Scott told Stan.

"I'm glad. Dad has been almost a basket case since Mom died."

The waitress whispered in Elana's ear and Elana said, "Dinner's ready. Let's move to the dining room. Sit anywhere you'd like."

Isaac and Kathy sat beside each other and whispered and giggled during the entire meal.

After dinner they all went back to the living room and were served pie and coffee as they enjoyed small talk.

The catering staff cleaned up the dining room, put the leftover food in the refrigerator and packed up the dishes and trash. When everyone was through with desert, they took those dishes and packed them in with the other dirty dishes. When they left, one couldn't tell there had been a dinner party except for all the food in the refrigerator.

"I think we're going to have enough food for the next week," Scott said. "Does anyone want a doggie bag?"

Elana gave each of the workers a fifty dollar bill as a tip. They thanked her profusely and left with a smile. She knew she would be using them again for future parties so she wanted to be sure they were happy too.

Before he left, Isaac made plans to take Kathy sight-seeing the next day. "I'll pick you up at 1:30 and have you back after we have dinner," he told her.

"That would be wonderful. What should I wear?"

"Whatever you feel comfortable in but wear comfortable shoes. I'll be wearing shorts and a tee shirt with sneakers," Isaac told her. "Oh and bring a camera if you have one."

"I've got one on my cell phone, will that be okay?"

"That'll work. See you tomorrow."

After they had left, Megan and Darren went up to their apartment and Scott went upstairs to read for a bit before going to bed.

Elana and her mother sat on the sofa and talked for a while.

"Do you think it's okay to go with Isaac tomorrow? It's not a date or anything," Kathy asked.

"I say go and make it a date. Mom, how long has it been since you enjoyed the company of a man, a gorgeous man," Elana teased.

223

"He is handsome, isn't he," she said as she blushed slightly.

"Go, have fun."

"It will be fun, I've been staying in way too long."

"Let's get to bed, we can look at the bible tomorrow. You need some beauty sleep and lots of rest for tomorrow."

"I'll lock up and turn out the lights," Elana said as her mother started up the stairs.

"Looks like Mom has a date tomorrow," Elana told Scott.

"Looks that way, glad they hit it off. Isaac seems like a nice guy."

"He does and I haven't seen that glow in Mom's eyes for a long time."

Isaac had a whole week of events planned for him and Kathy so Elana spent most of the week alone at the house.

The next day as Elana was sitting on the porch taking a break from her internship studies the old woman appeared.

Elana looked at her and said, "I wish I could communicate with you."

To Elana's surprise, the old woman smiled and said, "Follow me."

"Okay," Elana said surprised. She got up and followed the old woman towards the school.

When they were about half way there, Elana noticed three log cabins to her left and to her surprise, the small house and carriage house were gone. She looked back and her house was gone too. *What the ...,* she thought but she kept following the old woman even though she was starting to feel terrified.

The old school didn't look old and as they turned the corner to the front of the building she saw several horses tied to a hitching post. Above the porch was a sign that read Belle's Place. They walked up the steps to the front door and Elana heard talking and music coming from inside.

She looked in and saw the staircase but it was in excellent shape and had a young girl and man going up to the second floor. There were tables on the right side of the room. At one table there were two men and two girls sitting and laughing. The girls were all dressed in beautiful dresses. At another table was an older woman, probably in her thirties, sitting alone with an open book and a pencil. Along the back there was a long bar with a handsome young man wiping glasses.

To the left were several sofas with girls or girls and men sitting and talking. In the back corner near the bar was a very young dark skinned girl sitting and reading.

"See the woman at the table alone," the old woman said.

"Yes," Elana replied.

"That's Belle, the woman who owns the place. The dark girl in the corner is Lucy and the man behind the bar is Sam."

"Oh my god, that's my grandmother! Can I ask your name?"

"I'm Sarah."

As soon as Sarah told Elana her name, she disappeared and the old building shifted back to the present leaving Elana standing alone on the porch.

Did that just happen or was I dreaming? She looked back into the school and saw an old pencil on the floor where her grandmother had been sitting. She went in a picked up the pencil and carried it back to the house. She was surprised when she picked it up because it still felt warm from the last person that touched it.

Chapter 22

Elana put the pencil on the stand in the foyer so she could show to her mother and tell her about what she had seen.

Later that same afternoon, Sarah came back to visit Elana.

"Hello Sarah," Elana said when she saw the old woman.

"Child, there be evil around here and you, your man and your friends have been chosen to rid it of the evil," Sarah said.

"How can we do that?" Elana asked. "We've never dealt with anything evil before."

"You must follow what I say and the evil can't hurt you."

"What is the evil?" Elana asked.

"It be the spirits of the three men the girl killed at the hog pen. They seek revenge on the anniversary of their deaths each year. Some years no one is around and they get angry."

"What can I do?"

"Follow what I say or you will all surely die," Sarah said as she slowly disappeared.

"Don't go, I don't understand," Elana pleaded.

Elana sat on the porch for a long time thinking about what the old woman had told her and wondered what she was going to have them do. She could hardly wait for Scott to get home to tell him. She had wanted her mother to stay but now she was glad she wouldn't be staying long. It wouldn't be safe to subject her mother to unnecessary danger and she would want to participate no matter how dangerous.

Isaac brought Kathy home just before Scott arrived. Megan and Darren got home about an hour later.

"Honey, I have to go back home early. Isaac is driving me to the airport tomorrow. Hope you don't mind," Kathy beamed.

"Oh, Mom, you just got here," Elana complained.

"I know but Isaac is leaving and I do have lots to do at home. He's going to fly to Florida in a couple of weeks and spend a few weeks to see if he might want to move there."

"That's terrific Mom. I'm happy that you've found someone to spend some quality time with."

"Me too. He isn't your father but he's fun to be around and I really need someone right now. We're going to help each other trace our family trees."

"You do have a lot in common, especially this place." Elana wanted to tell her mother about seeing her grandmother and the inside of the brothel but decided against it just now.

After they went up to bed, Elana told Scott about Sarah's visit.

"What do you think she is going to have us do?" Scott questioned.

"I don't know but I think she thinks it might scare us. I think it's something we have to do or the evil spirits could track us down."

"This is getting pretty wild," Scott confessed. "I don't know if I'm up for this. I can deal with a ghost but not so sure about evil."

"We have to be if we're going to be free of them. Sarah said if we didn't get rid of them we might all die and I believe her."

"Okay, but I'm not sure Darren and Megan will go for it, especially Darren."

"I don't think they have a choice in the matter. I wonder what connection they have to this place."

"I don't know, but let's get some sleep. What time is your mom leaving tomorrow?" Scott asked.

"I'm not sure, Isaac is taking her and he's going to fly down to Florida for a few weeks to see if he might want to move there. Sounds like it might be getting serious. I just hope he doesn't hurt her."

The next day was Friday and Megan, Darren and Scott had all left by 9:00. Kathy had her bags packed and sitting in the foyer ready for Isaac to pick her up.

"I'll call when I get to the condo and let you know I made it okay."

"That would be great," Elana said as she hugged her mother.

"Looks like Isaac's here," Kathy said as she went to open the door.

They hugged and Isaac gathered up her bags and put them in the trunk of his car. Elana and Kathy hugged each other, cried a little and kissed each other' cheek before Kathy pulled away and ran down the steps to Isaac's car. Elana was so glad her mother was finally having fun after all these years.

She waved as they drove down the drive towards the road. Her mother acted like a teenager on her first date.

When they were out of sight, Elana saw Sarah once again.

"There's a full moon next week. On the night of the full moon, you, your man, and both your friends must perform a special ceremony out behind the carriage house," Sarah said.

"I don't know about going out there after dark. It's bad enough in the daytime."

"They can't hurt you after dark. They be afraid of the dark. I've put protection necklaces on your friend's night stands. Make sure they put them on. They will protect them."

"I will," Elana said.

"Be behind the carriage house at 10:00 on the night of the full moon and I'll tell you what to do. Follow what I say!" Sarah said just before she disappeared.

"Oh shit, this is too much!" Elana screamed.

She looked at the calendar and the full moon was next Thursday. She hoped she could convince Scott, Megan and Darren to follow her even though she wondered if it was crazy. *What if Sarah was just as evil as the spirits and was tricking her.* She didn't know what to do. She was afraid to do what Sarah was telling and afraid not to.

Her phone buzzed that she had received and email. She looked and saw it was from her old friend Katie.

Hi, Elana, I'm going to be in town and would love to meet up with you if you're free. Email me or call me at 555-345-6613. Katie

Elana emailed back with her phone number and told her she would love to see her. Maybe she could tell her what she should do.

A few minutes later Elana phone rang.

"Hi Elana, Katie here."

"Hi Katie, sure good to hear from you."

"I'm coming into town tomorrow for a conference and would like to catch up with you if you're free."

"Sure, what time?" Elana asked.

"I should be at my hotel around three so once I get checked in I'll give you a call."

"Why don't you stay with me and Scott? We have a big old house with lots of room and it would be fantastic to spend the evening catching up. "It will give you more time to meet my ghost too."

"I'd love to. I'll cancel my reservation and get back to you."

"Great. This will be so much fun. We haven't talked in ages."

"Call you right back," Katie said.

A few minutes later Katie called back. "Where did you say you and Scott moved to?"

"We bought a plantation out on Highway 2 outside of Cantor. It is awesome and like I told you the other day, it's haunted. Are you sure you don't want to rethink cancelling your reservations," Elana laughed.

"No way, I love haunted places. I'm anxious to get there and look your place over to see what might be there."

"Is Kurt coming with you?"

"Not this time, he's in Boston until next Thursday."

"Scott will be disappointed. Call me when you get in town and I'll give you directions."

"Will do. This is so exciting," Katie squealed.

The next afternoon Katie called and Elana gave her directions. She drove into the driveway about 45 minutes later. After parking her car, she climbed the steps to the porch.

"Come in, do you want a drink or something?" Elana asked as she held the door for Katie. "Scott and Darren will get your things. I fixed up a room with a private bath for you upstairs."

"This place is beautiful."

"I know, I couldn't wait for you to visit," Elana said. "I just love it here." She couldn't wait to tell Katie about Sarah's plan to get rid of the evil.

"Once you told me about the whore house and the ghosts, I had to visit."

They went in the living room where Scott, Darren and Megan were sitting.

"Hey everyone, this is my friend from college, Katie. Katie, you already know Scott. This is Megan and Darren. They're helping us with the renovations and Megan is going to go into business with me when we open our couples retreat."

"Hi Scott, great to meet you Megan and Darren."

"Hi Katie," they all said at once.

"I'm going to show Katie to her room. Scott, could you and Darren bring her things up?"

"Sure, toss me your keys, Katie."

When they reached her room, Katie asked, "what about the hauntings?"

"I'll give you the full run down after dinner."

"Do Darren and Megan know about them?"

"Oh yes and they are pretty much okay. I think Darren is more concerned than Megan and with good reason. I'll tell you all about it later."

"This room is perfect," Katie said as she looked around the room. "The house is fantastic. I can't believe you and Scott have bought a plantation."

"Me neither but it sort of fell into our hands and I feel I was destined to be here. I sure hope you can visit often and bring Kurt along."

Scott and Darren brought her luggage in and placed it at the foot of the bed.

"I think I'll freshen up and bit before dinner," Katie said.

"We're having pizza and salad for dinner as soon as the pizza delivery gets here."

"Sounds good. I'll be down in a little while. I'd like to grab a quick shower and change into something a bit more comfortable."

After Scott, Darren and Elana left Katie got out some comfortable clothes and took a quick shower. When she got out of the shower, she looked into her bedroom and saw an old woman standing beside her bed.

"Can I help you?" she asked as she wrapped herself in a towel.

After a few seconds the old woman disappeared. *I wonder what she wanted, she looked friendly enough.*

Katie got dressed and went down stairs just as Elana was paying for the pizza.

"Good timing," she said to Katie. "We'll eat in the kitchen and then Megan and I'll give you the grand tour before it gets dark."

They all made small talk while they ate and then Scott and Darren went into the living room to watch a TV. Megan and Elana cleared the table and started the dish-washer.

"Let's show Katie your house and the old school now and then we can give her the tour of this house after dark," Elana said to Megan.

"I'll get the keys and be right with you."

Elana and Katie went out the kitchen door and Katie said, "I had a visitor in my room a bit ago."

"Who," Elana asked shocked.

"I don't know, it was an old woman who just stood there smiling before she finally disappeared."

"That's Sarah, our resident ghost," Elana laughed nervously. "I hope she's friendly. She has told me we have to follow her directions to get rid of some evil that is centered on the property. I'll tell you all about it later and get your opinion."

"I feel she is friendly. She's been to my house too. I wonder why?"

"What?" Elana said.

"Yes, she was in my house a while back."

"That's strange. We really have a lot to talk about."

"So what is that old building down there?" Katie asked pointing to the old school.

"It used to be a school for young women and before that a whore house and before that a glebe house complete with church," Elana told her.

"Get out of here," Katie exclaimed. "Who owned the whore house?"

"Would you believe my great, great, great grand-mother?"

"What was her name?" Katie asked impatiently.

"Isabella but she went by Belle," Elana said. "Why?"

"Remember me telling you about finding the grave of a Confederate soldier in our back yard?"

"Yes."

"Well, she talked to me and she had an Aunt Belle who ran a whore house during the Civil War. The Confederate soldier was actually a girl who posed as a man to try to find men who murdered her family."

"No shit," Megan exclaimed.

"No shit," Katie said. "Supposedly the three men that killed her family came to the whore house and she tortured them and then pushed them into the hog pen for the hogs to finish off and eat."

"Let's go back to the house," Elana said. "We can do the tour another time. I want Scott and Darren to hear this."

They turned and walked back to the house. Darren and Scott were in the kitchen getting a beer so Elana turned off the TV so they could talk.

"Hey, why'd you turn that off?" Scott asked when he returned.

"You have to hear what Katie has to say," Elana said solemnly.

"OK, the game was over anyway."

Darren walked into the living room and Megan motioned for him to sit beside her.

"Do you want something to drink before you start, Katie?" Megan asked.

"No, I'll have a beer later."

Katie told the guys what she had just told Elana and Megan. "I think this is the place my Confederate soldier was telling about and if you have evil ghosts, they are the spirits of the three men."

Elana spoke up then, "There have been three deaths that we know of around the date the three men were killed. From what I've read and what you've said, I think the spirits are evil and are causing the deaths."

"We can't be sure about any of this but the evidence is quite alarming," Megan said.

The guys just sat there with a stunned look on their faces as the girls talked.

"When did the deaths happen?" Katie asked.

"One was this August. The real estate agent fell down the front steps and cut her throat on a boot scraper and bled to death. Darren found a wrecked car with a skeleton in it out in the field. It turned out to be another real estate agent who was here for an open house last August. I don't know if it's related but the previous owner's mother-in-law went crazy in August a few years ago. She died a couple of weeks later...in August," Elana said.

"According to my ghost, she killed the men in August in 1863. That's quite a coincidence don't you think. How does the old woman figure in?" Katie asked.

"She was a slave woman who was here at the time. She is sort of our protector right now," Elana told her.

"She was in my room earlier and she appears to be friendly so it makes sense that she is a protector."

Elana went on the tell Katie about what she had read in Lucy's journal and her grandmothers bible.

"I wish I could stay longer, this is fascinating and I'd love to help."

"I wish you could too but I'm sure we can handle this," Elana said even though she was skeptical and really wished Katie could stay.

"Oh my, look at the time," Katie said looking at the clock on the mantle. "It's almost 2:00. I really need to get some sleep. My conference is at 9:00 in the morning."

"Okay, let's turn in and finish this conversation tomorrow evening," Scott said.

"I'm afraid I have to leave after the conference but I'll be in touch to hear more about this," Katie told them.

Chapter 23

"What are we going to do about this?" Scott asked Elana when they finally in got into bed.

"I have a plan but it could be dangerous but I think if we don't do it we might all die."

"That's morbid, what's the plan?" Scott asked not really wanting to know.

"Sarah is going to help us," Elana started.

"You mean the spirit, how can she help us?" Scott asked.

"She has known these spirits for years so I think she will protect us. She told me we should go out behind the carriage house at 10:00 at the full moon and wait for her instructions."

"And we're supposed to believe a ghost?"

"I think it's the only chance we have."

"And she wants us to go out there after dark and confront three evil spirits?" Scott said in disbelief.

"She says they are afraid to come out at night so that's our best chance and she said if we don't get rid of them now, we could all die."

"I have my doubts about this. How do we know it isn't an evil trap? We'll tell Megan and Darren but I'm not sure they will go for it."

"We don't know but we might not have a choice. Sarah says they could track us down no matter where we go. We have to convince Megan and Darren but I'm so sorry I got them involved," Elana pleaded.

"Yeah, me too, and it won't be easy to convince them but we'll try. When's the full moon?"

"This coming Thursday."

"Shit, that doesn't give us much time to plead our case. I just hope we can convince them. I'm not even sure I'm convinced."

"I think Megan will be receptive but Darren can be pretty stubborn especially if he's scared."

"I'll talk to him," Scott said. "I think I can persuade him."

"Okay, let's get some sleep. Love you," Elana said as she kissed him goodnight.

The next morning, Scott carried Katie's bags down to her car and she left for her conference.

"I'll talk to Darren this afternoon while you talk to Megan. I have to run into work this morning for a few hours." Scott said as he got ready to leave for work.

"Hi Mom, what's up," Elana answered her phone on the second ring.

"I have some information for you that I think you might be interested in hearing," Kathie said. "I don't think finding and buying your plantation was accidental, I think it was fate."

"What, why do you say that?"

"After I got home, I called my genealogy research team together and we did some quick checking and found that all four of you kids have some sort of tie with that property. You know your tie Caleb and Belle's daughter. Megan is their son's great, great, great granddaughter and Scott and Darren both come from Sam's grandfather's line. How's that for a coincidence?" Kathy said with obvious pride.

"Wow, that's awesome. What prompted you to do the research?"

"Sarah."

"Sarah?" Elana questioned.

"Yes, your ghost. She came to me the first night I was there. She told me all about the evil spirits and that you all were chosen to remove them. It frightened me at first but I have confidence that Sarah will protect you. Just follow her instructions. It appears that it's equally important for all four of you to do this," Kathy said. "You were all chosen to get rid of the evil so do what you have to do and be careful"

"Oh Mom, I'm so frightened and I'm not sure Darren and Megan will go along with anything they think might be dangerous. They were so eager to live here but they might not be now."

"They'll need convinced, that's why I did the research. If they realize they are part of this too, they will be more receptive to getting rid of this evil."

"I hope so."

"I have to go now, Isaac is flying in this afternoon and I think he's going to move in with me."

"That's the best news I've heard in a long time, I'm so happy for you."

"Me too. I'll email a copy of the research to you this morning so you can show it to the others and be safe."

"I will Mom and thanks. Love you."

"Please be ever so careful and do exactly as Sarah tells you. I love you too. Bye."

When Elana got the email with the research she printed off two copies, one for her and Scott and one for Darren and Megan. She hoped this would convince Megan and Darren of what they had to do.

That afternoon, Megan came into the living room where Elana was sitting and showed her two boxes she had found on their night stands.

"Did you put these on our night stands?" she asked Elana.

"No, what is it?"

"It's two necklaces," Megan answered. "One has my name on it and the other has Darren's. They're strange but beautiful."

"I didn't put them there but I know who did. Sarah."

"You mean our spirit, Sarah?"

"Yes. They're for protection against evil spirits," Elana said as she pulled her necklace out to show to Megan.

"You have one?" Megan asked in astonishment.

"Yes and so does Scott."

"I don't know if Darren will wear it but he might since Scott is."

"He has to wear it!" Elana said. "He doesn't have any choice!"

"Here come the guys so we'll see," Megan said.

"Hey Meg, whatcha got there?" Darren asked looking at the boxes.

"Necklaces for us to wear."

"What! I'm not wearing a necklace," Darren laughed.

Scott looked at Elana and then at the necklaces Megan was holding. "I think you better wear one of these," he said to Darren. "I have one on and I'm glad I do."

"I don't know, I don't wear necklaces," Darren complained.

"Come with me," Scott said as he walked towards the front door.

"Where we going?"

"Out to the carriage house."

"Okay," Darren said.

One the way out Scott explained to Darren about the evil spirits that was on the property and that if they didn't have protection from them they might die like the real estate agents and who knows how many others.

"Okay, your freaking me out," Darren complained. "Dammit, I want to sleep at night but if you keep telling me this stuff, I just don't know."

As they got closer to the carriage house, Scott felt his necklace starting to vibrate. The closer they got the harder it vibrated.

"Feel this," he said as he pulled Darren's hand to the necklace.

"Whoa, what's happening?"

"It's vibrating because we are getting close to where the evil spirits are. They can't hurt me as long as I'm wearing this."

"All right, I'm convinced but it better work. I thought all we had to do was leave every August."

"I don't think that will work, it seems these spirits could track us down wherever we go."

"Now that's really freaking me out. What the hell have we gotten into? I didn't sign on to get killed."

"Me neither but it looks like we might have to follow through with this if we are ever to have any peace from these spirits."

"What the hell did we do to piss them off?"

"I don't know," Scott said as he shook his head.

They went back to the house and Megan and Darren each put on their necklace. As soon as they closed the clasp, a bright red light followed by a blue light surrounded them and then disappeared.

"What the hell was that?" Darren asked.

"Your field of protection was activated so now we have to get rid of these spirits."

Just then Elana's phone rang. She looked at caller ID and said, "it's mom, I have to answer it."

"Elana, are you sitting down?"

"Yes, what's up?"

"I just found that your father's line is related to the preacher who had the old school built."

"What, that's amazing and unbelievable."

"You've been connected with that place from the git go."

"Send me the research so I can look it over."

"I'll send it tomorrow. Isaac just got here about an hour ago. He's showering so I decided to call and tell you the news."

"Whenever you have time. Sounds like you're going to be busy for a while," Elana laughed. She really wished her mother was with her right now.

"I hope so. It's been pretty boring down here all alone. Gotta go, love you, bye."

"Bye, Mom."

"Okay everyone, listen up. It seems we are all related in some way to people who lived here a long time ago. Mom sent me some research she did and it seems we are the ones who will have to get rid of these spirits," Elana said as she handed the research papers to everyone.

"Well isn't this a hoot," Darren said. "We're all connected in some way. Guess that makes us property kin folk."

"This is just too strange," Megan said. "But it's sort of exciting for us all to be related to someone who used to live here."

"Do you have a plan on how we can get rid of the spirits?" Darren asked.

"I do. Sarah told me we are to go out behind the carriage house Thursday night at 10:00 and follow her instructions."

"Wait a minute, a spirit wants us to go out there after dark and battle evil spirits. There's something really wrong with this picture," Darren said slightly irritated.

"She says if we don't we might all die," Elana pleaded.

"I don't know, what do you think Scott?"

"I'm scared shitless but what else can we do? If we don't do something, come next August any or all of us could be killed."

"We'll think about it," Darren said taking Megan's hand. "This is way too much for my mind to process all at once. You're telling me we have to battle something that happened a long time ago just because a spirit tells us to. I could understand a living person telling us to do something about another living person but not spirits that we can't even see."

"I've already made up my mind," Megan said. "I'm doing it. I don't want to live in fear the rest of my life. They drove Mr. Jenkins' mother-in-law crazy and then followed her and killed her."

"We don't know that that's what happened," Darren argued.

"We don't know that it didn't either," Megan came back.

"All right, but I'm doing it under protest. I don't want to be called a coward," Darren said.

"So it's settled, we're going to kick these evil spirit's asses this Thursday," Elana laughed nervously.

"Looks that way," Scott said. "Let's have a beer."

"Let's get shitfaced," Darren laughed.

"Sounds like a plan," Scott said as he headed for the kitchen.

"Before we do, walk out to the carriage house with me and Megan. I want to test these babies," Darren said as he touched the necklace on his neck.

As they got near the carriage house the necklace on each of their necks started to vibrate. The closer the got the stronger the vibrations.

"Okay, I'm convinced. Let's get drunk," Darren said as he turned to go back to the house.

Later that night, Elana told Scott about her mother's phone call. "I can't believe I'm related to everyone who's lived on this property. I wonder what we'll find when we start renovating the old school. I hope there's no spirits, especially evil ones," she laughed nervously. "I've about had my fill of spirits, especially evil ones."

"Me too. I've had my fill of them for one lifetime," Scott said in all seriousness. "Once we are rid of these spirits, I'll be happy."

The days leading up to Thursday were tense to say the least. Everyone was on edge and tempers were short.

247

Everyone seemed to want to argue over the most insignificant things. When Thursday finally arrived, they were no longer talking to each other. Megan and Elana were sleeping in the spare bedrooms and Darren and Scott spent most of their time in their bedrooms.

When everyone arrived home Thursday afternoon Elana decided enough was enough.

"Okay everyone, we're adults here and we're all scared but that's no reason to be acting like children. Let's go down to the Chips and Chowder, have a nice civil dinner and then come back here and do what we have to do," she said as if her patience had finally run out.

Everyone laughed nervously and agreed that they should do just that. They all had a group hug and told each other how sorry they were for acting so childish. In the end both Megan and Elana were crying and laughing at the same time.

They had a leisurely dinner and got back home around 9:00. Scott and Darren sat on the front porch looking out at the carriage house while they waited for time to start.

"Well old buddy, do you think we are going to still be alive in the morning?" Darren asked with a worried look on his face.

"I sure hope so. I never pissed off an evil spirit before so I don't know what to expect out there but I'm glad you're going to be right there with me," Scott said.

"Yeah, me too. I wouldn't have let you do this alone. And we are property kin folk and best friends after all.

I guess we all inherited these spirits. Just wish we didn't have to be the ones to get rid of them."

"I guess we did so we have to stick together. I think after this is over we should look at some ground for you and Megan to build a proper house on. What do you think?" Scott asked.

"That would be great. I'm going to ask Megan to marry me when this is over."

"Fantastic. I get to plan the bachelor's party."

"And be my best man," Darren said.

"Here come the girls, it must be time," Scott said.

"Ready," Elana asked.

"As we'll ever be," Scott and Darren said at the same time.

"Let's do it," Megan said as she started towards the carriage house.

The moon was bright and they had no trouble seeing. The carriage house loomed ahead of them and the trees behind it cast eerie shadows that seemed to move to and fro.

Darren let out a small whistle when he saw the shadows. "Those are shadows and not the spirits aren't they," he asked.

"Yes, Sarah said the spirits are afraid to come out at night," Elana said.

"Hooray for small miracles," Darren laughed nervously.

When they got near the carriage house their necklaces started to vibrate. The closer they got the harder the vibrations.

Sarah was waiting for them when they got to the back side of the building. Darren and Scott stopped in their tracks when they saw her. They hadn't seen her before and were astonished that they could see her now. She smiled at the group and all at once their necklaces stopped vibrating.

"Oh shit," Darren said. "My necklace isn't working."

"It's working dear," Sarah said. "The spirits are quiet because I'm here."

Scott and Darren looked at each other and back at Sarah. They couldn't believe they were seeing and talking to a ghost.

"You must follow my directions or you will die," Sarah said. "Do you understand?"

"Yes," they all said together.

"Take hands and form a circle around the rock crevice over there. Whatever you do, do not, I repeat, do not let go of each other. If you let go, you will be sucked down into the crevice and die. Do you understand?" she asked.

"Yes," they all said together.

"Scott, take Elana's hand and start walking around the crevice. Elana take Darren's hand and Darren take Megan's hand. When you are completely around the crevice, Scott you take hold of Megan's hand to form a circle. Do not let go of each other no matter what happens! Do you understand?"

"Yes," they all said again.

As soon as they were around the circle, their necklaces started to vibrate violently. The ground started to shake and the crevice started to open. The noise was deafening. Then they heard laugher, evil sounding laugher.

"Do not let go of each other!" Sarah screamed.

Soon their necklaces vibrated so violently that they fell off their necks and into the crevice.

The laughter quickly changed to blood curdling screams. The rock crevice opened a bit more and three black shadows flew out one by one then they flew back inside, screaming the whole time.

The ground shook violently and the roar was almost unbearable.

Megan started to weep and Darren was sweating profusely but they held tight.

After about five minutes, a fire ball burst out of the crevice barely missing the four in the circle.

"Oh my god, it's deafening and I'm so scared," Megan screamed.

"Don't let go!" Sarah shouted.

Soon the screams grew silent and the flames retreated back into the crevice and finally burned out.

The earth closed and the crevice disappeared. The entire ordeal only took about 15 minutes but to those involved, it seemed like an eternity.

Sarah was still standing and watching and she now had a smile on her face. "It's over," she said. "You can let go of each other. The evil spirits have been sent back to hell and won't bother you again unless the gateway is opened again. As long as you live here, be careful not to dig in this spot."

They all looked over at Sarah and saw an old man was at her side and what appeared to be angels were all around them.

"This here is Jake, he's come to fetch me," Sarah said as she looked lovingly at Jake. Jake smiled and took Sarah's hand as they were encased in a brilliant blue-white light.

"We be leaving now," Jake said as they disappeared into the brilliant light.

"Holy shit," Darren finally said, "that was scary. I damned near pissed my pants."

"I thought we were going to be sucked into the ground," Megan said.

"Well, I'm glad it's over," Scott offered. "Darren, what do you say we have this all covered with cement so no one will ever dig here again. We won't even level it, just have a cement mixer drop a whole load and smooth it out."

"The sooner the better. I don't want that gateway ever opening again."

Elana was silently crying and didn't say anything. She felt it was her fault her husband and friends had to go through this but was glad they were there with her.

When they got to the front porch Darren turned to Megan, "Megan, we just kicked evil's asses together so will you marry me?"

252

"What!" Megan screamed. "Yes, I'll marry you!" She grabbed him and kissed him so hard they almost fell down.

"This calls for a drink," Scott said as he took Elana's hand and went in the house.

They all got beers and sat around the living room recounting the excitement they had just endured.

"I think we should get married this weekend," Darren offered. "What do you think, Meg?"

"The sooner the better. When you come down from this high you might change your mind," she laughed.

"Never, I've been waiting for the right time to ask you ever since we came out here. When I thought we might die tonight, I knew I didn't want to wait any longer."

"Megan, I've offered Darren some ground any place you all want to build yourselves a proper house if you want it," Scott told her.

"Oh that would be wonderful! Our very own place right here near you all," she squealed.

"Scott, that's a fabulous idea," Elana exclaimed.

"Why don't we all play hooky from work tomorrow and make a long weekend of it?" Scott suggested. "I have some comp time coming, what about you Darren?"

"I can get off if you girls can."

"I don't think we'll have a problem, after all, we are working for free," Megan said.

"Let's drive in town to the Silver Ring and have some fun then," Scott said.

253

They all piled into Scott's vehicle and drove down the drive to the main road.

As the drove past the old school, a door creaked, a mist floated into the room and a rocking chair started rocking.

In the hidden cellar beneath the kitchen a figure paced back and forth in the inky darkness. It paced from an alter in the middle of the room to the stone steps leading up to the kitchen. Behind one of the doors in cellar room a red glow filtered through the cracks. Soft whispers, sobs, moans, and an occasional growl could be heard.

Meet J. Thayer McKinney

J. Thayer McKinney lives with her husband in a log home in the mountains of eastern West Virginia. She is a wife, mother, grandmother and great-grandmother. She and her husband are the owners of Cedar Loft Productions, a small publishing company. She is a writer and a paranormal researcher.

She loosely bases some of her fiction books on her paranormal research. So far, she has not encountered many malevolent spirits but before she does research she grounds herself for protection. "You can never be too careful with the unknown!" she says.

She is an ordained minister and holds a PhD in Metaphysical Parapsychology. She has also earned a Bachelor's degree in Business Administration and an Associate's degree in Electronics.

Prior to retiring from the corporate world, she had a very successful and rewarding technical career. She managed the IT department at a healthcare facility and prior to that position she was an industrial controls technician and a telecommunications technician for a power company.

When she isn't writing or working at her publishing company, she enjoys traveling, ghost hunting or sitting on the front porch listening to the sounds of nature.

Read J. Thayer McKinney's previous novel

Grave Vengeance: Esther's Story

Willy held me as I died in his arms. "Why'd ya do it Essie, I'd have taken care of you," he sobbed. I watched as he lowered my body in the grave and covered it with dirt then rocks. I so wished I could make him hear me.

After I died, my spirit was held on earth drifting between longing to be with Willy and my family once again and unimaginable loneliness. I had no perception of time, seasons came and went, each day and night was like the one before, filled with nothingness.

I was so happy when a couple moved into the house that had been built near my grave. Once they moved in, I decided to explore the house. The first thing I noticed was a calendar on the kitchen wall. I couldn't believe what I was seeing. The date said August 2013. *I've been dead 150 years!* I began to weep because I knew everyone I had known were long dead.

Was what I'd done so horrible that I was to wander around this place forever?